GODDESS OF DEATH

CLOCKWORK THIEF BOOK SIX

KATHERINE BOGLE

Patchwork Press

http://katherinebogle.com

Cover Design by Ravenborn Covers

First Edition — 2019

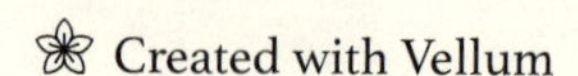

GODDESS OF DEATH

CLOCKWORK THIEF
BOOK SIX

KATHERINE BOGLE

THE KNOWN WORLD

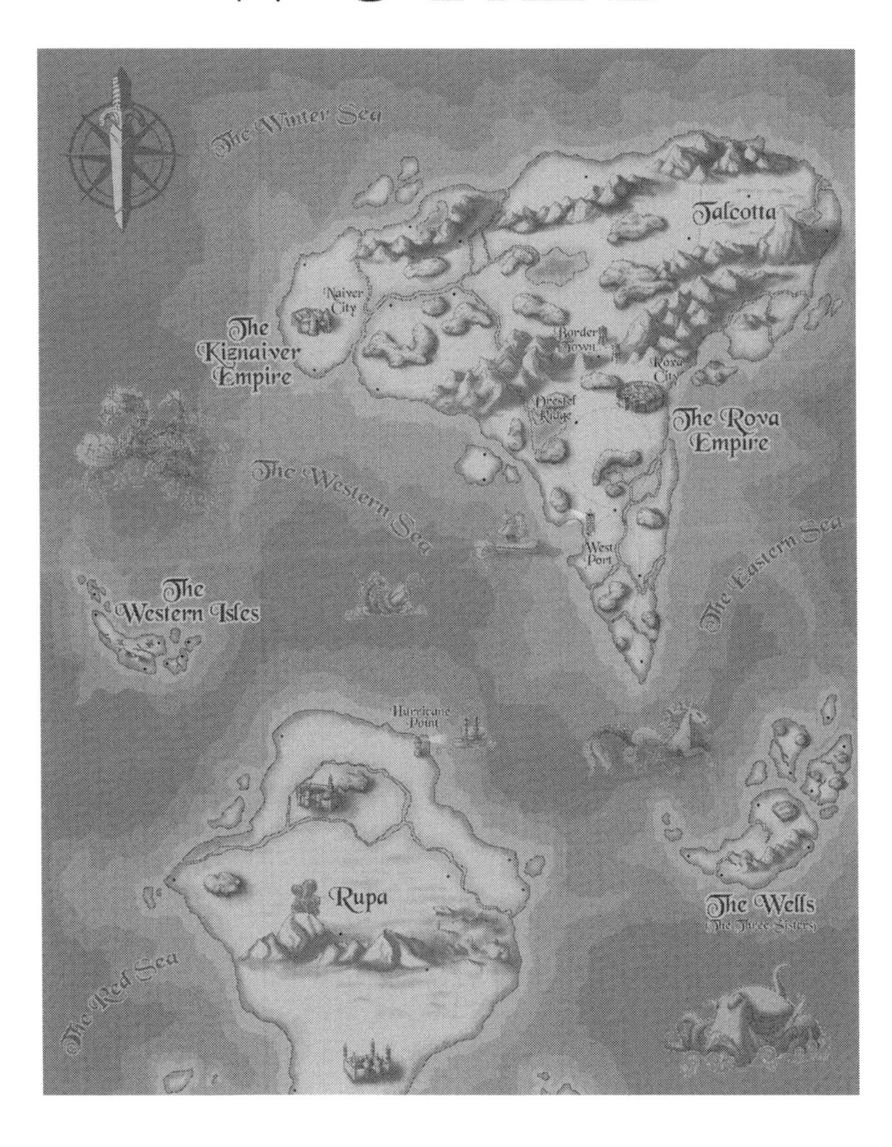

Narra groaned as she pulled herself back into consciousness. She blinked, her eyelids heavy as the world came back into view. The darkness holding her receded a fraction, letting in the harsh whisper of voices and the feeling of the ground shaking beneath her.

"She's waking up again," a male voice said.

Her pulse pounded in her skull, giving her a splitting headache to go with the pain hindering her every breath. She reached for her head with one hand and clutched at the linen bandages wrapping her stomach with the other. What in Srah's name was happening?

"Rheka," a familiar voice rumbled.

For some reason she thought the tone of his voice strange, like it should be monotone instead.

"What?" she rasped. Her throat hurt too. Great. Just another thing to add to the list of many.

The ground bumped beneath her and pain shot up her spine as something hard dug into her back.

"Where am I?" Narra asked. She tried to sit up, but dizziness gripped her in its claws, forcing her back down onto the uneven ground.

"In the back of a steamwagon," the voice supplied.

A steamwagon? Narra opened her eyes again, not realizing she'd closed them. She looked up into dark eyes fringed by inky hair.

"Clint?" Her eyebrows furrowed in confusion. She had to be dreaming, but what kind of bizarre dream was this? She was quite certain she'd never dreamed about the Commander of Shadows before.

Clint nodded. His forehead was wrinkled and his eyes kept darting to the side like he was looking for something. When Narra tilted her head up to see what the hell he was so interested in, she caught the gazes of Mika and Dom.

"I'm dreaming, aren't I?" she asked.

Mika rumbled a laugh. "Do you dream about lying on three men often?"

Lying on... The thought wouldn't fully form. As she leaned up to see what Mika was talking about, she realized why the ground beneath her was so uncomfortable. She was lying over the laps of Clint, Mika, and Dom. All three of them were wedged into the back seat of a steamwagon.

She should be embarrassed. Her body should heat, and she should scramble to get away—but she didn't. The pain was too much, and it brought back memories.

Memories of a razor-tipped whip and an empress with white hair flashed through her mind. She'd been in the middle of a fight, and she'd been about to win. But just as her sword had descended to claim Danicka's life, a boom had filled her ears. Then she'd fallen to her knees.

She'd been shot. Someone had fucking *shot her*.

"It's far more fun when you react, sweetheart," Mika grumbled.

Ignoring the assassin, Narra turned to see who drove. Asher's hands wrapped around the steering wheel, his knuckles white and his eyes narrowed at the road. Dark curls tumbled over the seat on the right side, and then dark eyes flecked with gold met hers.

"Narra," Avalon whispered as she turned in her seat. Therin, who sat between the general and the pirate, gave her a look.

"Avalon," Narra whispered. She reached out for the pirate, but pain speared her gut, making her inhale sharply.

"Stop moving," Clint said. "You're going to make it worse."

Narra hesitated before slowly letting her hand drop back onto her belly.

Avalon smiled ruefully and reached out to brush back Narra's hair. Another bump in the road nearly made her smash her head off the ceiling.

"Enough," Therin snapped. "Turn around and sit down."

Avalon glared at the lieutenant, making the man wince. Even as Therin leaned away from her, she obeyed, slipping back down to sit.

"I was shot," Narra said. She felt like she needed to say it out loud to make it real. She'd been stabbed, cut, and gutted before, but she'd never been shot.

"You were," Clint said warily, like he didn't know where she was going with this.

"It fucking *hurt*," she added.

Clint's lips twitched in a small smile and he shook his head. "I don't imagine it would feel pleasant."

"I don't recommend it."

Clint chuckled. "Good to know."

"Am I going to live?" Narra asked no one in particular. She was in pain, exhausted, and felt like her body could give way at any moment, but she didn't feel death's embrace like she had the night Asher had tried to kill her.

Clint avoided her gaze.

"Of course you are." Mika snorted. "You wouldn't be my little death bringer otherwise."

Narra groaned, making pain tear through her stomach. She winced. "Enough with the nickname."

Mika grinned. Before he could speak again, Asher cut him off.

"You're going to be fine," the general said. "We'll reach Rova City in the next few hours and find you a healer."

A healer? Right. She might need one of those.

Darkness crept across her vision again. She realized this hadn't been the first time she'd woken. Though every instance blurred together, she knew it was true. How long had they been driving for already? How many hours could she last?

A thought sparked at the back of her mind. There was one person who could help her—one who she'd gone to in the past. Ria.

Before Narra could voice her thought, blackness closed around her.

"Her breathing is growing faint," someone said.

Narra started back into consciousness, sucking in air like she was starving. "What's going on?"

"We're nearly there," Clint said. "Try to stay awake."

Narra nodded numbly. Distantly, she realized the pain was gone. Everything felt fuzzy, and looked even worse—like a haze lay across her eyes. She tried to blink it away, but it stuck like a thin film over her vision.

Her eyelids grew heavy again. Why did she need to stay awake? Sleep sounded so nice right now. She closed her eyes to give into the darkness.

"*Rheka*," Clint growled. "What did I just say?"

She blinked her eyes open again. "Stay awake."

"Right."

Someone squeezed her arm—probably in an attempt to keep her conscious. She hardly felt the pressure, and soon her eyes were drifting closed again.

"Death bringer," Mika warned.

Narra opened her eyes. It was so dark around her. No wonder she was having a hard time staying awake. She wasn't sure when night had fallen. It seemed just as dark as the last time she'd been awake.

Oh yes. She had been awake before.

Last time, she'd been trying to remember something. There was something she needed to do. Her eyebrows furrowed as she tried to push through the fog muddling her brain.

"You need to hurry, Grayson," Clint snapped.

"I'm going as fast as I can," Asher said defensively.

"Then go as fast as the steamwagon can. I don't care how fast *you* can drive."

Darkness pushed in on the edges of her vision, blurring Clint's face even further. She blinked lazily, trying not to fall back into unconsciousness while simultaneously digging through her brain for what had been so important.

Something in her chest burned suddenly, and she nearly sat up when her stomach roared with pain. Narra cried out. Stars flew across her vision.

"I thought I told you to stop moving," Clint grumbled. He held her shoulders down as she panted.

"Ria," she said before she forgot again. "I need Ria."

Clint's eyebrows furrowed. "Ria?"

"Yes," Narra snapped even as black stars encroached on her vision.

"Who is Ria?"

Before she could answer, the stars consumed her sight, pulling her back into the void.

A DOOR SLAMMED, wrenching Narra from unconsciousness. She breathed heavily as she tried to sit up, only to have pain steal her senses.

"Narra," Asher whispered. "I'm here. You're going to be all right."

Her forehead wrinkled in confusion as she was dragged from the back of the steamwagon and cradled against the chest of the next emperor. Her cheek pressed against his cold armor. He hadn't even changed before they'd left? That must have been a long, uncomfortable drive.

"Where are we?" Narra asked weakly.

She couldn't feel much of anything. After the spark of pain inside the steamwagon, everything returned to numbness.

"The palace," Avalon answered. The pirate's head popped into view, her forehead wrinkling with worry.

"You're going to be fine," Asher said.

Narra wasn't sure whom he was trying to assure, her or himself.

Her body was shifted and jostled slightly as Asher bounced up the front steps of the palace. The front doors were wrenched open by two startled looking guards.

"Your Majesty!" they gasped in unison.

Asher barely grunted a hello as he raced through the open doors and began tearing through the castle. "I need a healer!" he bellowed.

The pound of boots told her they were being followed. How many had been in the steamwagon anyway? She couldn't remember who was all there.

"Have a healer sent to my chambers at once!" Asher roared. He continued through hall after hall—everything a blur until they reached the third floor royal suites.

Narra's eyebrows furrowed as she wondered when they'd arrived there. It normally took so much longer to get through the palace, but it seemed like only seconds had passed.

"Open the doors!" Asher snapped.

"Yes, s-sire!" a guard stuttered as he flung the doors to Asher's chambers open.

Asher stormed through the council chambers to the other side of the room. The doors cracked against the wall as he kicked them open to reveal his bedchamber.

"Where is that damned healer?" he rumbled. His chest vibrated against her cheek. She wished he didn't have all that armor on. It was so cold with her body pressed against it.

Her mind drifted back to a night where warmth had enveloped her in Asher's arms. She closed her eyes to savor the moment. She was sure these had to be her last. She was far too tired to ever wake up again.

Something soft rested below her, making her eyes flash back open. She was lying in Asher's bed, a soft comforter puffing up around her. She wanted nothing more to sink into it and close her eyes.

"Try to stay awake," Asher said gruffly. A warm hand pressed against her cheek, and fingers brushed back her hair. "You've got to stay conscious as long as you can."

Narra couldn't even think of anything to say to that. She leaned her face into the warmth, a small smile pulling at her lips. She couldn't remember why they didn't want her to sleep, but she knew she wasn't supposed to.

The warmth drifted away, making her whine slightly.

"I'm right here," Asher assured her.

"What was she saying in the car?" Avalon asked.

"Something about a person named Ria," Clint answered. "I've never heard of them."

Avalon's gasp made Narra's eyes flash back open. *Wait, Ria!*

"The Daughter!" Avalon said. She threw her hands up in the air as she spun to face Narra. She kneeled on the floor next to the bed and clutched Narra's hand.

"Ria," Narra said. Her thoughts slowly clicked back into place. She needed Ria. Ria could heal her.

"How do we find her?" Avalon's eyes sparkled with hope.

"What's going on?" Asher snapped.

"The daughter?" Mika asked. "She has a kid?"

"No," Clint said, though even he sounded unsure of himself.

"Narra," Avalon urged.

Narra turned her gaze back on the pirate. It was *so* hard to focus. "Ria. My pocket." Her fingers inched for the leather pocket strapped to her thigh.

Avalon stood and leaned over Narra's legs. She quickly unzipped the pocket and pulled out the red beads Ashra had given Narra. The pirate dangled them over Narra's chest. "Is this what you need?"

"What in Srah's name are those?" Asher asked.

"Shut up!" Avalon snapped. She glared at the rest of them. "Just let her concentrate."

Narra blinked hard, trying to hold onto consciousness. If she could call Ria, she would live. The assassin would fly across the city to find her. She could get through this. She just had to stay awake.

"Wrap them around my wrist," Narra instructed. She called to mind her lessons with the goddess and the assassin. "Put the moon in my palm."

Narra barely felt her hand being jostled or the cold beads pressed against her skin.

Avalon gently folded Narra's fingers around the moon. She squeezed quickly before leaning back. "Now what?"

"I call her," Narra said. She closed her eyes and pulled on the rage inside of her. With everything as cold as ice, it was difficult to find a spark of fire.

"Don't let her go to sleep," Asher snapped.

"I'm not!" Avalon growled. "Be quiet!"

When silence lasted for too long, she heard the others shift.

"Someone needs to find Erik," Avalon whispered.

"Right," Clint said.

"Hurry."

Narra's forehead wrinkled. She tried to tune out the voices and focus on her memories. She pictured the rage she'd felt when Asher had stabbed her, but her anger over that was long gone. She tried thinking of her father and all he'd done to her, but again, she had moved past that. Her fingers tightened on the moon until the edges bit into her skin. She thought of her mother and heat flared inside her. She wasn't sure she'd ever forgive Khlara for trying to take the Guild from her. She deserved to run for the rest of her life—to be hunted by Mika and his comrades.

Warmth licked her palm, and gasps sounded around her.

Ria, she called into her mind. She pushed through the numbness and the haze, focusing on the one thing she could do to save herself. *Ria*.

"What's going on?" someone snapped.

"Silence!" another person growled.

Narra squeezed her eyes shut as tightly as she could. "*Ria*, this is hardly the time to play coy."

Cold slithered across the edge of her mind, like pinpricks of ice spearing her brain. It should have hurt, but instead, it made her smile. *Ria*. She'd heard Narra's call.

"She's coming," Narra whispered before darkness took her.

A crash brought the world around her swirling back to life. Narra gasped and leaned up on her elbows in time to see Ria hit the floor and roll before springing to her feet.

The assassin growled as she prowled around the bed, putting herself between Narra and the men protecting her. Asher, Therin, Dom, and Mika branded their swords, but their surprise quickly faded as they realized Ria had put herself between them.

"Who are you?" Asher snapped. He motioned at Ria with the tip of his blade.

Ria's lips pulled back in a snarl as she withdrew her sword. "None of your concern." Her gaze flicked to each of the men. "Which one of you hurt my sister this time? I will *end you*!"

Narra tried her best to sit up. She had to get this situation under control before it escalated. Her breath hissed out as she pulled on her injury, but she managed to get herself leaned up against the pillows and the headboard.

"Narra," Avalon whispered. "Are you all right?"

The thief nodded. She barely had the chance to register Avalon sitting on the bed beside her, almost glued to her side, because she was so focused on what Ria might do next. "Ria," Narra said. "Don't hurt them."

Ria shot a glance over her shoulder. She paced back and forth between the bed and the four men. "Which one of you was it, hm?"

"Ria!" Narra snapped. "It wasn't any of them. The man is dead."

Finally Ria stopped. She turned to look at Narra without turning her back on the men. "I swear to Ashra, if you're lying to me Narra, not even Lady Death will be able to stop me from killing the man that hurt you this time."

Narra's lips twitched in a small smile. She'd always thought Ria didn't like her, but the assassin really did seem to care about her. "I promise you, the man who shot me is dead."

Ria snorted. "He's lucky, then. He'd have prayed for death at my hand." She glanced down at Narra's stomach and her eyes widened slightly. She rushed to close the space between them, her hands hesitating over Narra's wound. "Sister..." she said on a breath. "How do you keep getting yourself in these situations?"

"A lot of bad luck," Narra grumbled.

Ria's lips twitched before her expression faded back to fury. She glanced angrily at the four men slowly lowering their swords before looking back at Narra. "I won't always be around to save you, Sister."

"I know," Narra said.

"Who is this?" Asher snapped as he stepped forward. "When Avalon said 'the Daughter,' she didn't mean—"

"The Daughters of Ashra," Ria cut him off. She narrowed her eyes at the soon-to-be emperor, taking her time sizing him up.

Therin scoffed. "They don't exist."

Ria rolled her eyes. "Then who am I?"

"You can argue later!" Avalon cut in. "You healed her once before, didn't you?" She glanced down at Narra.

Ria nodded. "Yes."

"Then do it again," Avalon demanded. "Before she dies."

Ria regarded Avalon for a long moment before she slowly dipped her chin. She pulled an identical set of beads from the confines of her cloak and dangled them over Narra's stomach. Before she could continue, her entire body stiffened. Ria looked at the four men beginning to inch closer.

"You will come no closer if you know what is good for you," Ria threatened.

Therin and Dom blanched at the threat, while Mika smirked at the challenge. Asher simply narrowed his eyes.

"Listen to her," Avalon growled.

The men exchanged looks before nodding and backing off. They hovered at the edge of the room, looking between Narra and Ria.

The assassin snorted at their suspicious looks, then turned back to help Narra. She carefully unfolded Narra's hands from the injury and cut away the linen. Blood dripped down Narra's skin, and she shivered as the hot sensation broke through the cold.

"This is going to hurt, Sister," Ria said.

Narra stiffened. "I remember."

"Then I'll begin."

Narra braced herself as Ria closed her eyes and took up her chant. The beads glowed almost immediately followed by the blackening of the moon.

Pain crashed through the numbness that had settled over her skin. Narra snapped her teeth shut on a cry of pain and arched her back as it worsened.

It felt like a dozen knives were sliding in and out of her skin, pulling out the last pieces of shrapnel not removed by the healer while simultaneously stitching closed each of the small wounds littering her abdomen.

Her heavy breaths were the only sound competing with Ria's chants. Sweat poured down her forehead, and Avalon grabbed her hand. Narra squeezed her fingers like her life depended on it.

Her entire body burned with pain for what felt like hours. At last, the knifing sensation dulled to pinpricks, and then she could finally breathe again without wanting to wail. Her eyelids fluttered closed as Ria's chanting died off.

Ringing filled her ears. It took her several minutes to get her breath back. Once she had, she could feel the weight of her body pressing into the comforter. Her hold on Avalon slackened, and then it was Avalon squeezing her fingers tightly.

"Is it done?" Avalon asked, worried.

Narra smiled and forced her eyes back open. Though the pirate had been addressing Ria, she only looked at Narra.

Avalon smiled when she caught Narra staring and leaned down to kiss Narra's forehead.

"It's done," Ria said. She stepped away from the bed, darting a glance at the four men inching closer again. "If I find out any of you had anything to do with this, I don't care what Ashra says, you *will* die."

"You speak of the Goddess of Death as if she was real," Mika said slowly.

Ria stiffened, and her assassin mask fell firmly into place. Narra had a feeling that Ria didn't slip up often.

"She is," Narra said, earning a glare from Ria. But she was too tired to play coy, or pretend things that existed weren't real. She hated the lying, especially to those she cared for.

"Narra," Ria warned.

Asher stepped closer, forcing Ria's intense gaze away from Narra. If the assassin were a cat, her hackles would have definitely risen. The general caught Ria's look but continued to move closer anyway, clearly having no survival instinct.

"Ria," Narra said softly. "They won't hurt us."

Ria didn't look away from the general. "I'm sure that's what you thought before one of them stabbed you three times." She narrowed her eyes at Narra. "Remember that, Sister. Trust gets you killed."

"It can also save your life," Narra said.

Ria clenched her fists. "Narra, let me take you away from these people. They don't deserve you."

Narra couldn't help but chuckle. Ria was right in a way, but she also had it all wrong. Narra didn't deserve *them*, not the other way around. At Ria's questioning look, Narra only shook her head. "I can't."

Ria sighed. She looked between the four men slowly approaching and the window. "Fine." She twisted her jaw before slowly making her way around the bed to the windowsill. "I don't trust these people, Sister. Come find me when you've rested."

"I will," Narra promised.

Ria ducked out the window and disappeared into the night before anyone could say another word.

Once the assassin was gone, the four men returned to the bed. Their eyes widened with surprise as they took in the small scars marking Narra's stomach. The raised silvery skin was barely visible through the blood still covering her.

Her cheeks heated with embarrassment. She was getting tired of people she didn't know well seeing her skin.

"She actually healed you," Asher said, sounding surprised. But his eyes weren't glued to the small scars that the gun's shrapnel had carved into her. Instead, he looked at the three scars that were the width of a dagger.

"It wasn't the first time," Narra said quietly.

"Ashra is... real?" Mika asked. He sounded skeptical and worried all at once.

Narra sighed. Her body was still heavy with sleep, but she had a feeling they weren't about to let her relax anytime soon. "Yes."

"How is that possible?" Dom asked.

"How is healing a gunshot wound in minutes possible?" Narra countered.

"Magic," Avalon said. She squeezed Narra's hand. "If I

can control the weather, and Ria can heal such a terrible wound, why can't the gods be real?"

"*Gods*, as in... more than one?" Therin paled.

"Let's not go that far," Avalon said. "We're only speaking of Ashra right now."

"So the Goddess of Death is real?" Asher clarified, finally meeting Narra's eyes.

She gulped the lump in her throat. She had no idea how they were going to react to this. "Yes."

"And you're... one of her assassins?" Asher continued.

Narra nodded.

"I knew you couldn't be a simple thief," Mika said. "But I hadn't imagined this."

"I was only a thief when I nearly killed you," Narra said, smiling.

Mika narrowed his eyes, but before he could respond, Asher cut in.

"He tried to kill you?" The general's hand clutched the hilt of his sword.

Hot rage slammed into her chest. He couldn't be serious. "Yes," Narra said. "And he isn't the only one in this room either."

The others exchanged looks—all but Avalon, who didn't remove her gaze from Narra. The pirate knew exactly what she was talking about. In fact, Narra had confessed everything to her long ago.

Asher cleared his throat. "So how long have you been an assassin?"

Narra sighed and leaned back into the pillows cradling her head. "A few weeks, maybe longer."

Asher worked his jaw. It was clear he wanted to say more—to ask her questions about when and how this had all happened—but he kept his mouth shut in front of the others.

She was grateful because all she wanted to do right now was sleep. Just as she was about to sink down into the comfort of the bed, the window slammed open again. Narra groaned and opened her eyes to find her best friend stepping off the windowsill.

Her eyes widened and she straightened immediately, sitting up as Erik raced around the edge of the bed.

"Erik." She had to be dreaming. There's no way he could be real.

Erik fell to his knees at the side of the bed. He grabbed her hand and squeezed it hard. "You're alive! Clint said you might be dead by the time we returned."

The Commander of Shadows appeared at the edge of her vision, having slipped in right after Erik.

"I'm alive," Narra said. Tears burned the back of her eyes. "I'm sorry. I'm sorry for everything."

Erik shook his head. He stood quickly and folded her into his arms. "No. I'm the one who's sorry." His hot breath bathed her hair as he pressed her against his chest. "I should have let you explain. I should have listened."

She couldn't hold the tears back any longer. They burned down her cheeks as she squeezed her friend in her arms. "I understand why you didn't."

Erik hugged her tighter. "I'm so glad you're okay."

Narra chuckled darkly, her voice almost hiccupping on a sob. "As okay as I can be."

Erik started to laugh too. "You've got to stop doing this to yourself, Narra."

"I know," she said. "I'm thinking of taking some time off from nearly dying."

Erik stiffened and his grip tightened almost painfully. She could barely breathe, but it might have been the best she'd ever felt. Erik was back. He was *here*, and he was holding her. He didn't hate her anymore, or at least she hoped.

"That sounds like a good idea," Erik said, his voice hitching.

Narra buried her face against the cold of his cloak and breathed in the smell of home.

Narra pulled from unconsciousness for what felt like the thousandth time in the last twenty-four hours. She blinked slowly, pushing away the haze of sleep while continuing to bask in the heat wrapping around her.

She sighed blissfully and snuggled up against that warmth threatening to pull her back into the black behind her eyelids.

Soft breathing tickled her cheek, forcing her eyes open again. She blinked in surprise at Avalon, who lay curled up against Narra's side. The pirate was wrapped around the thief—her mess of curls was tucked into Narra's neck and her leg was draped over Narra's. She was sleeping soundly, her chest rising and falling rhythmically.

"Good morning," Erik whispered.

Narra's cheeks heated as she turned to look at Erik. Her best friend sat in an armchair at her bedside, his hands folded in his lap and dark circles under his eyes. Avalon might have finally gotten some rest, but it seemed the same couldn't be said for Erik.

"Good morning," Narra said quietly. She glanced down at Avalon, but the pirate didn't stir.

"You've developed quite the little following," Erik commented. He looked at Avalon before flicking his gaze at Mika, who sat in an identical armchair next to the fireplace. The assassin dozed, his head lolling back to lean against the backrest.

Narra smiled ruefully. "Some are more appreciated than others."

Erik caught her meaningful stare and smiled. He leaned forward and took her hand, squeezing it between both of his. "I'm so sorry, Narra. I should have been there for you."

Narra shook her head. "There's nothing you could have done."

Erik glanced down at her stomach, which was covered in dried blood. "Maybe."

Narra squeezed his hands to get his attention. "Truly. The entirety of the army surrounded me. If they couldn't do anything, no one could have."

"The entire army?" He raised an eyebrow.

Narra's lips twitched. "I may have strayed onto the battle-field a little more than I intended."

"Somehow that doesn't surprise me."

Narra narrowed her eyes and went to hit his arm play-fully, but to do so, she'd have to remove either her numb arm from under Avalon or her other hand from Erik's grasp. She wasn't willing to give up either one, so she remained still instead.

Erik chuckled softly. "All the same, I'm sorry. I should have let you explain yourself."

Narra's heartbeat sped up. This was her chance. Finally she'd get to tell him what had really gone on. "I told Asher I delivered the death of a thousand cuts myself. I did it to protect the Guild. We need that alliance."

Erik's eyebrows rose. "You told him you tortured his son alone?" She nodded. Erik squeezed her hand. "No wonder he tried to kill you."

Narra shrugged her unoccupied shoulder. "He is sorry. I can see the guilt in his eyes every time he looks at me."

Erik stiffened. He avoided her gaze while slowly working his jaw back and forth. "That doesn't forgive what he did."

"I know, but I forgave him. That's what matters."

Erik slowly met her gaze. "I don't like it. He deserves to die."

Narra opened her mouth to protest, but Erik shook his head.

"He deserves it, but it isn't my justice to serve. I don't like that you've forgiven him, but I won't try to kill the general again," Erik said.

Narra sighed in relief. "Thank you."

"Will you forgive me too, then?" Erik's cheeks flushed, making Narra grin.

"Oh, I don't know. You said some very rude things to me," Narra said.

Erik blanched.

Narra barely stifled her laughter. She bit the inside of her cheek and took a deep breath to keep her body from shaking. One glance at Avalon confirmed the pirate was still asleep. "I'm teasing," she said.

Erik narrowed his eyes. "Very funny."

"I thought so."

Erik's gaze strayed to the pirate. "That seems to be going well." It was Narra's turn to blush. "You know she stayed up half the night watching over you. She only gave into exhaustion a few hours ago."

Narra's face burned with embarrassment. "I like her."

Erik snorted. "I know that." He smiled. "She seems to like you as well."

"I think so too." Narra couldn't fathom why, but the pirate seemed to have grown quite attached to her.

"I'm happy for you," Erik said. "Does this mean things are over with Grayson?"

Her embarrassment faded to a deep well of sadness she didn't realize she possessed. Slowly, she nodded. "Yes. It's for the best."

Erik nodded. "I agree. You don't need him."

Narra smiled sadly. "I know. But I wanted him."

Erik shifted awkwardly. "Sometimes these things just don't work out."

"What else did I expect when I got involved with the next emperor, hm?"

Erik squeezed her hand. "Enough of this. Why don't you update me on what I've missed?"

Narra's shoulders relaxed. She was grateful for the change in subject. "Right. You're probably wondering who that is." Narra nodded at Mika's softly snoring form.

"The thought had crossed my mind."

"That's Mika. He's one of the Talcotta assassins after my mother. He followed a lead back to me on the battlefield. He's refused to leave my side for more than a few hours since. He's got it in his damn head that my mother will reach out to me at some point."

Erik rolled his eyes. "He clearly doesn't know your mother."

Narra grimaced. "Not at all."

"And what about the battlefield? How did the gunshot happen?"

Narra winced. Erik was not going to like this. "Well... Empress Danicka of Kiznaiver, who we believe wields some kind of spirit magic her crown, challenged Asher. I was his bodyguard, so of course, I couldn't let that happen."

"Of course," Erik said dryly.

"*So*, I stepped in. She's a brilliant fighter, but she's not as brilliant as me."

Erik chuckled. "Still so humble."

"Always." Narra flashed a small smile before she continued. "I was about to kill her when one of her soldiers stepped out of line and shot me to protect her."

Erik's eyes widened. "Truly? The empress must have been grateful for that."

"She was furious. She killed the man in front of everyone."

"Whoa."

"I was surprised too," Narra admitted. "But she did give us two days reprieve for her soldier's slight."

"That's generous."

Narra tilted her head as she thought back to it. "She seems like a very honor-bound woman."

Erik raised an eyebrow. "That's a bit extreme, though."

"How much do you know about Kiznaiver culture?"

He shrugged. "Not much."

"Me neither. Maybe they really are that different from us," Narra reasoned.

"It could be." Erik stared into the fire on the other side of the room as he thought.

They lapsed into silence—the easy, comfortable kind that Narra had missed in his absence. She rested her body back into her pillow, staring at the closed doors leading to the council chambers. She assumed everyone had gone off to take a break, get cleaned up, and figure out what their next steps were.

Narra looked forward to cleaning up as well. Her clothes had a grungy feel to them. She shifted as she realized how many of her weapons poked into her.

She sighed and closed her eyes, thinking back to her fight with Danicka. The *boom* of a gun echoed in her mind, making her open her eyes again. Still, the sound seemed to reverberate in her ears. She could barely remember what had happened next. There had been shouting, and people had tried to care for her. At some point she'd been hoisted up onto a horse and taken back to camp.

Then everyone had been surrounding her, and she'd been in *so much* pain. A healer had come, but she'd thought Narra would die. Little had the old woman known that Narra didn't go down easy.

Her heart skipped a beat as she finally remembered the

last thing she'd heard before she had given into the darkness dragging her under. A messenger had charged into the tent with a message from the palace.

"Marina has escaped," she whispered feverishly. Narra jerked and began to sit up when she remembered Avalon was still sleeping against her. She shot a panicked look at Erik, her heart racing. "Marina has escaped!"

Erik nodded solemnly. He already knew. "We'll get an update soon, I'm sure."

Narra twisted gently, ready to swing her legs over the side of the bed and leave the blissful warmth of the woman beside her. But before she could get her legs out, the world tilted and dizziness forced her to still.

"Narra?" Erik untangled their fingers and gently pushed her shoulders back so she was lying down. "Don't strain yourself. Someone will return soon. I'm sure Grayson won't leave us for long."

She shook her head. "I need to know what's going on."

"And you will." Erik raised his eyebrows meaningfully. "But right now you need to take a break."

"But—"

"Shhh," Erik hissed. "Rest for a while. I'll wake you up when they return."

Narra narrowed her eyes suspiciously. She knew her best friend. If he thought getting some rest was the best thing for her, there was no way he would wake her up. "You promise?"

Erik grinned, flashing his teeth. "I promise."

Now that was a guilty look if she'd ever seen one.

Narra sighed and leaned back into the plush pillow. No matter how much she wanted to argue, that little dizzy spell was making her body feel heavy again. Maybe she could do with a few more hours of sleep. If Asher wasn't there, then there was no update worth knowing—or so she reasoned in her mind.

Before she'd made a conscious decision on what to do, sleep engulfed her once more.

Voices murmured nearby, gently waking Narra. For the first time in what felt like days, she woke up not feeling tired. Coupled with the leftover healing effects from Ria's magic, her body felt energized from all the sleep she'd gotten.

She reached out for Avalon, only to find the bed empty next to her. She blinked in surprise as she felt around before turning to verify her conclusion. The bed beside her was cold. Avalon must have gotten up some time ago.

She turned back around to look for Erik, but he was nowhere to be seen. Narra sighed and sat up, throwing off the blanket she didn't remember someone laying on top of her. Before she could swing her legs over the side of the bed, she caught Mika staring at her from his seat next to the fireplace.

The assassin smirked and tilted his head, which leaned

against his hand. He didn't say a word, only watched her with a knowing look in his eye.

Narra rolled her eyes before slipping out of bed. She paused to take in her surroundings. She'd nearly forgotten she'd been sleeping in Asher's bedroom. Instead of dwelling on that, she moved on to her next set of concerns. Where was everyone?

She turned to the double doors leading into the council chambers. That's where the voices were coming from. She counted them one by one until everyone but Clint was accounted for. Now that they were back in the city, she assumed he had returned to the Guild.

Narra smoothed out her clothes, which were still grimy and covered in dried blood. She scowled at the sight—another shirt ruined—before running her fingers through her hair. She was missing a few weapons, but found her sword, pistol, and grappling hook alongside a couple daggers atop the nightstand.

Good ol' Erik.

"Not going to say good morning?" Mika asked, pitching his voice low.

Narra turned to face him. Before she could answer, the palace shook and a *boom* filled her ears. She stood stock-still until the sound of the explosion died and the rattling of nearby objects ceased.

Mika shot to his feet, two daggers already in hand. Narra whipped around and raced through the council chamber doors, sending either door cracking against the wall.

"What's going on?" she demanded. Her heart pounded as she took in her comrades: Asher was cleaned and dressed in regular leathers; Avalon looked mussed but still gorgeous as always; Erik had not one hair out of place; and the two lieutenants staring at her with wide eyes.

"I don't know," Asher said as he raced to the door. He pulled it open and exchanged a quick word with the guard before he leaned back inside.

"Was that an explosion?" Avalon asked. "It sounded close."

"It was," Erik said. He knew as well as she what an explosion sounded like. Having the Boomers as part of the Guild had made them familiar with the sound long ago.

"We need to find out what's going on," Asher said. "Therin. Dom. Come with me." He turned to the door before Narra could catch him.

"Wait a second!" she hissed.

Asher hesitated with the door half open. "I'll be back." He gave her a meaningful look, but didn't wait for her response. He disappeared into the hall with his two guards watching his back. She hated that she wasn't with them. She wanted to know what was going on too.

"We should prepare to leave," Mika said.

Narra turned to find the assassin looking uncharacteristically serious. "We can't leave without Grayson."

"If there's going to be a fight for the palace, we need to go." Mika crossed the room and grabbed her bicep.

She yanked her arm free and grabbed a dagger, pointing it directly at his throat.

Mika chuckled darkly even as the tip of her blade brushed the underside of his jaw. "You got me again."

Narra growled. "Do not tell me what to do."

Mika nodded slightly, not seeming to mind how close her dagger was to killing him. He stepped back, holding his hands up in a defensive gesture. "Fine. We wait for your general, and then we go."

She nodded. "That's the plan."

Battle cries rang out somewhere outside, making her rush to the window. Narra slammed her palms against the windowsill and peered through the glass, but she couldn't see anything from this side of the building.

Her heart raced as she tried desperately to crane her neck and find some glimpse of the situation. All she could see was a wall guard racing towards the palace gates.

"The gates," Narra said. "Someone blew up the gates!"

"That'd make sense," Avalon said slowly, "if they wanted to take the palace by force."

Narra banged her fist against the glass. "Danicka. It has to be her. So much for two days of peace."

Avalon's forehead wrinkled. "It could be someone else."

"Who else could it be?" Narra spun around and began pacing between Asher's room and the council chambers. When she had enough of pacing and hearing the sounds of battle flooding the castle, she returned to the nightstand. She quickly strapped on her remaining weapons. She went to adjust her cloak when she realized it no longer clung to her shoulders. She'd forgotten Asher had removed it at the warfront.

Narra resumed her pacing, all too aware of the three sets of eyes tracking her movements. When a battle cry sounded out in the hall, she'd had enough.

Narra rushed to the outer doors and threw them open.

"Narra!" Avalon snapped.

Erik appeared at her shoulder, and they both leaned out to peer down the hall. The two guards stationed outside their door were no longer in position. Instead, they fought what appeared to be two Rovan mercenaries at the junction at the end of the hallway.

"What in Srah's name is happening?" Erik said under his breath.

She grunted her agreement and tore her sword from its sheath.

"Wait! Narra!" Erik called after her. But Narra was already charging down the hall.

Her legs pumped, pushing her faster and faster, but she wasn't fast enough. Both guards fell beneath the blades of the mercenaries, only getting in a few quick hits before they went down. With the two guards bleeding out on the floor, the mercenaries stepped over their bodies.

A set of green eyes met hers as a growl rumbled in her throat. She launched herself into the air, bringing her blade down on the throat of the green-eyed man. He spluttered as blood sprayed his comrade.

The second man barely had time to raise his blade before a throwing knife slammed into his chest. The mercenaries fell side by side.

Narra looked back at Erik, who was still positioned to throw a knife. "Thanks," she said.

"Anytime." Erik smiled.

"What's going on?" Avalon jogged down the hall to meet them, bringing Mika with her.

“I don’t know,” Narra admitted. “They look like mercenaries.”

“But they’re Rovan,” Erik said.

“So they aren’t Danicka’s men,” Avalon reasoned.

Narra shook her head. “I guess not.”

“Then who could it be?” Mika asked, sounding more curious than invested like the rest of them.

“A noble making a go for the crown?” Narra guessed. “I’m not sure what else it could be. We need to find Asher and the others and get out of here. The Royal Guard can handle it, I’m sure.”

Mika stared pointedly at the two dead Rovan soldiers. “*Riiight.*” He drew out of the work sarcastically.

Narra turned away from the trio and marched down the hall. Battle cries and the clang of swords continued to echo through the palace. This was a big battle—on par with the last one to take the castle. Nervous sweat dripped down her spine as she turned into the next hall. With no sign of Asher, Therin, or Dom, she turned back into the royal wing, heading for the servants’ staircase.

She led the way down the winding steps to the second floor, where the sounds of battle were far louder. A cry of pain cut through the air, followed by a gurgle of blood. Something hit the ground hard, and then Narra leapt into the hall.

“Asher,” Narra sighed in relief.

The general stood with his two guards, blood splattering their clothes and wild looks in their eyes. They looked back at Narra and the others as they stepped out into the hall.

“There!” someone shouted at the end of the corridor.

Narra looked away from the group to find a pack of mercenaries rushing their way.

"Get back!" Asher snapped. He turned to face off against them, but Therin and Dom stepped in his way. Therin parried the first man to leap at them while Dom took down the second.

Before Asher could break through and attack the third, Narra slid beneath the mercenary's legs and leapt back up to slice the throat of the next. Before she could get her bearings, a fourth attacker slammed his blade against hers.

Narra hissed out a breath in her effort to hold back the large man. He was a beast at least double her size with large hands and a wicked smile. His scarred face told her he'd seen many battles. So they really were mercenaries—probably hired to take the castle by force for someone with a trickle of royal blood.

She let the man push her back until victory flashed in his eyes. Once she saw that glimmer, a smirk pulled at her lips. He lost his smile the second she sidestepped him, letting him fall forward. She slipped around the side of him, cutting through his leather armor to slice through his ankle. He cried out as he went down.

She turned in time to see Mika plunging his sword through the man's skull. Narra acknowledged him with a nod before turning back to see how the others fared. At least a dozen mercenaries raced towards them.

"We need to go!" Narra snapped. She grabbed Asher's arm and yanked him back towards the staircase.

"We can't!" Asher pulled back, but she didn't loosen her hold.

"We must!" she argued.

"What about the palace?"

Narra scoffed. "What about it? An empire isn't a pile of brick and mortar. An empire is its army, its people, and its emperor. We don't need this damn palace." Asher blinked at her in surprise. She pushed him towards the staircase. "Go!"

Asher listened—probably for the first time since they'd met. While Narra guarded his back, Asher led the charge up the stairs, joined quickly by Avalon and Therin.

"I'll hold them here," Dom said. His eyes were locked on the approaching mercenaries, and his jaw was set. He wanted to give up his life to save them.

"No heroics today," Narra snapped. She yanked three throwing knives from her belt and exchanged a quick nod with Erik before returning her attention to Dom. "Go with your emperor. We'll take care of this."

Dom gave her a startled look. Then he laughed, and she was the one giving him a shocked look. "You were dying only yesterday."

Narra choked on laugh. "That was yesterday, comrade."

Dom nodded swiftly and dove out of the way. He disappeared up the staircase while Narra, Erik, and Mika were left to face the oncoming enemy.

"You really enjoy danger, don't you, death bringer?" Mika asked.

Erik snorted. "You don't know the half of it."

"At least I keep things interesting," Narra said.

"That you do." Mika chuckled.

The assassin shot forward first. Narra cursed under her breath as she raced after him. She threw her knives in quick succession, hitting one mercenary's eye socket, another one's chest, and a third enemy's shoulder. Two dropped dead, while the third slammed into the wall—her blade throwing him off balance. Another two went down from Erik's knives while Mika leapt on the first to reach him.

Mika spun in a graceful arc, his movements timed and almost choreographed like a dance as he sliced through each enemy with precision. Blood flew around him, spraying the walls, the carpet runner, and the surrounding paintings with red, while hardly getting a drop on his actual clothing.

Narra blinked in surprise. She was impressed by his display, even if she had managed to one-up him more than once.

She charged forward with Erik at her side, and together they took out the rest of the squad just as more shouts sounded nearby.

"*Ancestors*," Narra cursed.

"It's time to go," Mika said. He didn't try to grab her again, but he did stand directly in front of her and glare.

"Fine." Narra spun on her heel and led the way back to the staircase. The second they appeared on the third floor, more cries echoed in the nearby corridor. "We've got to get out of here."

"That we do," Mika agreed.

They raced back to Asher's room and dove inside. Erik slammed the door behind them and flipped the lock. He exchanged a quick look and then a nod with Mika before they began upending furniture to pile in front of the door.

"What are they doing?" Asher demanded.

Narra took a quick moment to check him over before she

did the same with Avalon, Therin, and Dom. Everyone was safe and alive.

"They're buying time," Narra said. "We need to get out of the palace."

Asher scoffed. "They're blocking our only exit."

Narra shook her head. "No, they're not."

She crossed the room and stood by the windowsill, unlatching the window before she threw it open. Cold air pushed her hair back and made her shiver. The smell of snow was in the air.

"We're on the third floor," Therin grumbled.

"Yes, we are." Narra withdrew her grappling hook and stepped up onto the ledge. She reached back to take whoever offered their hand first. She wasn't surprised when Avalon slipped her fingers between Narra's.

The pirate stepped up onto the ledge and Narra yanked her close. She wrapped an arm firmly around Avalon's waist before she aimed her grappling hook at the outer wall of the palace.

"I'll take you one at a time. When Erik is finished, he can lend me a hand," Narra explained. "Do *not* move when we're in motion. I promise not to drop you."

"Is this how you get into General Grayson's chambers?" Dom asked, sounding aghast.

Narra flashed them a smile. "Yes, but it's our little secret." She winked as she pressed down on her grappling hook. It shot forward in a burst of compressed air before wrapping around the head of a gargoyle. When she yanked the cord taut and it didn't budge, she prepared herself to fly. "Are you ready?"

Avalon nodded, though she had grown pale. "Let's get this over with."

Narra squeezed the pirate tight. She knew Avalon was afraid of heights, but this was their only way out, unless they wanted to fight their way through the enemy all evening.

"Hold on," Narra said. Avalon answered with a tightening of her arms.

Narra stepped off the ledge and hit the retract button. The cord propelled them over the courtyard, air rushing by them on all sides. Her pulse pounded with adrenaline until she removed her thumb from the button and they slowed before touching down on the top of the wall.

"Are you all right?" Narra asked.

Avalon nodded numbly.

"Can you keep an eye out while I get the others?"

Avalon took a quick glance around before nodding again. "I can do that."

Narra's heart squeezed. Despite how afraid Avalon was, she was being *so* incredibly brave. Narra pulled the pirate closer and gave her a quick kiss, barely a brush of lips before she stepped away and returned her grappling hook to her hand.

Avalon blinked at her in surprise. Some of her daze seemed to disappear just as Narra shot off her hook again.

"More of that later," Avalon said, a sly smile creeping up her face.

"That's a promise." Narra grinned before she hit the retract button and flew back over the courtyard the way she'd come.

She landed on the ledge and quickly stepped back inside.

Pounding echoed from the doors. Erik and Mika pushed against the tables and chairs they'd assembled, holding the enemy rattling the entryway.

"They're here?" Narra questioned.

Asher and his guards turned surprised looks on her. "You're back already?" the general asked.

Narra shrugged. "What of it?"

Dom stepped forward, urging Asher with him. "Take the general next."

Narra nodded. "Of course."

"Wait," Asher said. "This is my palace. I should be the last to go."

"Not gonna happen." Narra yanked Asher up onto the windowsill with her. "Like I said, you need to survive this. The rest of us don't matter."

"You matter to me," Asher growled. He gripped her forearms in his hands and squeezed. The intensity of his gaze caught her off guard, but she quickly shook her head.

"Then come with me now," Narra said. "You're only putting me in danger by wasting what little time we have."

Asher's eyes widened slightly. He hadn't considered that. After a long hesitation, he finally nodded. "All right."

"Hold on tight," she said.

She waited until Asher had slipped his arms around her. Her entire body heated at the contact. *This is not the time!* She shook her head and tried to focus as she shot her grappling hook out over the courtyard. Once it was settled around the gargoyle's throat, she looked up at Asher.

His lips were pressed into a firm line and a million thoughts seemed to fly through his eyes, but he didn't voice them. Instead, he simply nodded his readiness and squeezed her waist.

Narra sighed and faced the yard. She squeezed the grappling hook, holding on as tight as she could as it ripped them off the ledge. Asher's grip squeezed the breath out of her. Her ribs burned from the strength of his arms, but then they were landing and she quickly pulled from his hold.

She gasped in a few breaths before sending her grappling hook back across to the palace.

"Are you all right?" Asher asked at the same time Avalon approached, looking worried.

"I'm fine," Narra panted. "You just knocked the breath out of me."

"Apologies."

Narra shook her head. "Don't worry. I'm fine."

Before they could stop her, Narra was flying across the courtyard once more. When she landed on the windowsill this time, the door was cracking open, wood fragmenting to reveal the hallway beyond.

"Shit." Narra stepped into the room. "Erik and Mika, it's time to go!"

Erik looked back at her. "We can't carry two of them at once."

Therin and Dom turned terrified eyes on her.

Emperor's Ancestors. He was right. She could carry one, and Erik could carry another, but carrying two was out of the question. She'd just have to be fast, flying back and forth as quickly as she could.

"Don't fret, death bringer." Mika chuckled. "I can find my own way down."

Narra's eyebrows furrowed in confusion. "You can?" She inspected him for signs of a hidden grappling hook or similar device but found none.

"Trust me," Mika said.

Narra scoffed. "Never."

Mika scowled, but Erik didn't give him time to answer. He raced across the room, leaving Mika to curse and splutter as he tried to hold the door closed.

"Therin, you're with me," Erik said.

"And what if I want to be held by the gorgeous woman?" Therin asked.

Narra groaned. "Srah, please just smite me now."

"You're larger and more difficult for her to carry," Erik reasoned. He narrowed his eyes at the guard. "We don't have time for this."

"They're right," Dom said quickly.

"You're only saying that because you get to go with Narra," Therin said.

Narra narrowed her eyes. "Who gave you permission to call me that?" Her fists clenched at her sides.

Therin blanched. "Apologies, I heard the others—"

"I can't hold this for much longer!" Mika called from the other room, sounding strained.

"Come on." Narra climbed onto the windowsill and pulled Dom up with her. The guard tentatively wrapped his arms around her waist while his cheeks flushed and his eyes looked anywhere but at her. "Shy, are you?"

Dom cleared his throat. "Sometimes."

"You're going to need to hold on tighter than that if you want to survive."

Dom tightened his grip as Narra sent her grappling hook back across to the courtyard. "Hold on," she said.

Before Dom could answer, Narra hit the retract button. The guard yelped as they sailed through the air, the current pulling at every inch of their clothes and hair. They were only in the air for half a minute, but by the time they landed, Dom quivered from head to toe.

Narra carefully released him and retracted her grappling hook. "Are you all right?"

Dom nodded, though his face was going green.

"Flying isn't for everyone," she said.

Narra looked back across the courtyard as Erik and Therin flew through the air. She stepped aside, pulling Dom with her to make room for the next pair.

Before they landed, Narra caught sight of Mika slipping out the window. He inched across the ledge before leaping up to grab the overhang a foot above his head. Somehow he managed to pull himself up onto the roof before he climbed down to a drainpipe clinging to the side of the palace. He slid down it before trotting gracefully across the yard.

Two sets of boots slammed down on the wall beside her. Narra turned to find Erik releasing Therin, who was wind whipped and grinning like a fool.

"Holy emperor's balls, that was thrilling!" Therin said. He turned to share his amusement with Dom, but Dom was dry heaving over the side of the wall. "Didn't enjoy your ride, Dom?"

The other guard grunted and mumbled something obscene about Therin's heritage before Therin started laughing.

"What now?" Asher asked. He and Avalon approached now that they were all safe. "And where is your other friend?"

"Mika will join us shortly," Narra said. She glanced at the yard again but couldn't spy his shadow.

"Let's rappel down the other side of the wall, and then we'll head somewhere safe to collect ourselves," Erik suggested, already unspooling his grappling hook to tie it off.

"Good idea." While Erik went to work, Narra inspected the yard once again. Still, she caught no sign of Mika. Instead of returning to the others, she took in the palace. She could just make out a few battles, and a couple of dead bodies, in some of the windows.

Narra winced. Whoever had planned this, they had planned it well. It was the perfect time for a coup with the soon-to-be emperor and his army off at war. It was only bad timing that they'd all been inside when it happened.

A steamwagon turned up the driveway suddenly, pulling her attention from the building. Her eyebrows furrowed as she watched the lavish vehicle slow to a stop in front of the palace steps.

Narra slowly walked around the wall to get a better look, her heartbeat speeding up with every step. Cold dread sat in her stomach. She really hoped it wasn't who she thought it was.

As soon as the steamwagon rolled to a stop, the driver leapt out and rushed around the side. Mercenaries spilled from the front doors of the palace, widening to line the staircase and welcome whoever had masterminded this plan.

The driver opened the door to the steamwagon and offered his hand. Gloved fingers reached out and took his hand before the woman slipped out of the vehicle and onto the cobblestone driveway.

"Marina," Asher gasped. She wasn't sure when he'd come to stand by her shoulder, but she felt the heat of his closeness now.

"Marina," Narra echoed. Her lips pressed into a firm line as they watched the former empress.

Marina climbed the steps to stand in front of the palace doors. A smug smile sat on her lips as she turned to face her mercenaries. "Well done!" she called, loud enough for Narra and Asher to hear. "Victory is ours!"

"We need to head back to the warfront to gather aid," Asher whispered feverishly. Even as he tried to pitch his voice low, his words still echoed off the alley walls.

The group of them huddled between two buildings not far from the palace. After they had witnessed Marina take back the Imperial Palace, Mika had shown up and together they had rappelled down into the city. They hadn't gotten far before Asher had stopped them.

Narra could see all the thoughts running through his head. His eyes were wide, almost manic. His breathing had quickened and beads of sweat amassed on his forehead. He didn't deal with stress very well.

"Agreed," Dom said. After a few minutes of fresh air, Dom had perked back up, looking embarrassed for dry heaving over the palace wall. "We need to stop whatever is going on here."

"Then it's settled," Asher said. "We'll gather a steamwagon from my home in East Gardens and head back to the warfront."

"Wait!" Narra snapped. They were getting too far ahead of themselves. The warfront was a day's journey, less in a steamwagon, but so much could happen in that time. "I might have a closer option."

Everyone stared at her expectantly, making Narra sweat. She gulped the growing lump in her throat and took a deep breath to regain her composure.

"I can ask the Daughters for help," she said.

Everyone's eyes widened but hers.

"You can't be serious," Erik said.

"Would they truly help?" Asher asked.

"What about the Thieves Guild?" Dom inquired. "They might be a safer option."

In comparison to assassins, the Guild was safer—but there was no way they could raise an army to take back the castle. The Daughters, however, had magic. If Ashra agreed to help, they might be able to cut through the enemy like butter.

"The Guild can't help," Erik said. "We don't have those kind of resources after—"

Narra cut him off with a look. She didn't need everyone knowing the Guild's business.

"At least let me try," Narra said. "I can go meet with them and see if they can lend a hand. Erik, you can take everyone to my apartment."

Erik's eyebrows rose in surprise. "Your apartment? You

never let anyone go there." He shot a glance at Avalon, who looked surprised by this news.

"Desperate times." Narra shrugged. "I'll need a new place after all of this anyway. Take them. I'll meet you there in a couple of hours."

"Every minute counts, Rheka," Asher said. His gaze darkened.

She knew he was right. If this didn't pan out, they'd have wasted a few hours. But wasting a few hours was better than wasting an entire day travelling to the warfront if they didn't have to. Plus, the border *needed* those soldiers. They couldn't take that many of them away from the war just to reclaim the palace.

"I know," Narra said. "I'll be as fast as I can."

Asher held her gaze for a long moment before he nodded. "Go then."

"Be careful," Erik said.

Narra's lips twitched in a small smile. She nodded and then raced out of the alley. She hardly made it across the street before she heard footsteps behind her. She skidded to a stop and spun to face Mika, who sported a lazy grin.

"What do you think you're doing?" Narra asked. She narrowed her eyes at the assassin.

"Where you go, I go." He shrugged.

"Srah help me." She closed her eyes and took a deep breath before opening them again. "You know where I'm going. I can't take you with me."

"Sure you can." Mika winked as he meandered by her into another alley.

"I *can't*." Her heart raced at the very idea. Bringing Mika to see Lady Death would be a death sentence for them both.

Mika must have heard her change in tone because he stopped and turned to face her. His forehead wrinkled and the amusement dropped from his face. "You're not just going to see the Daughters."

Narra ground her teeth. "No."

"You're going to see Ashra?"

She could strangle him. "*Yes*," she hissed.

Mika regarded her suspiciously. He still didn't believe that the Goddess of Death was real.

"I don't have time for this." Narra stormed by him and withdrew her grappling hook from her belt. Before she could shoot it off, Mika grabbed her arm and threw her up against the wall.

A dagger was pressed against her throat, the cold edge nipping at her skin before she could even blink. Somehow, she wasn't surprised. Narra glared at the assassin. She didn't like being caught off guard.

Mika smirked, but it was devoid of all humor. Somehow the smile became menacing. "You really expect me to believe that Ashra is real?"

Narra bit her tongue on an exasperated groan. "No. I don't expect you to believe it, but it's true."

He raised an eyebrow. "Do you believe she's real?"

Mika watched her face with strange intensity. His gaze flashed everywhere—from her eyes, to her cheeks, to her lips, and to her nose. He was assessing her for a lie, she realized.

"I know it," Narra said.

Mika's jaw hardened. He knew she wasn't lying. "You believe her to be," he clarified.

"No. I've seen her with my own eyes," Narra growled through her teeth. Every moment here was a moment wasted. She needed to get to Ashra's cellar and find out if the goddess would help them.

Mika stepped back, looking startled and a bit disconcerted. "I don't believe you." He returned his dagger to his belt while Narra rubbed her throat.

She sighed. "That's fine, but stop hindering me."

Narra turned on her heel and marched down the alley. She hated turning her back on him a second time, but if she'd just proven anything, it was that Mika wasn't going to hurt her. He could have many times. But he didn't. He really believed her mother might reach out to her at some point, and he was going to keep her alive until that happened.

NARRA LANDED on the grass on the other side of the stone wall circling the manor that housed Ashra's cellar. Her heart raced with her anxiety. If it wasn't enough that she was about to ask a *huge* favor of the goddess that told her to stop asking for favors, she had to drag along the most irritating assassin she had ever met.

Mika hit the ground inches from her, flashing his usual smirk. However, something dark had settled in the assassin's gaze, and his customary amusement was gone, replaced with something forced.

"Wait here," Narra said. She straightened and took a step towards the open cellar doors.

"Aren't I invited?" Mika asked.

Narra glared at the man. He wasn't taking this seriously. "If you enter that cellar, we both die."

Mika's smirk fell. "And how do I know you won't slip away while I wait out here?"

"It's a *cellar*," she said, motioning at the blackness between both cellar doors. "There's nowhere to go."

Mika looked between her, the house, and the cellar. After an agonizingly long minute, he nodded. "Fine. I'll wait here."

Thank Srah.

Narra dipped her chin before she turned back to the cellar and descended the steps. The darkness was heavier than usual in the basement. There was hardly any purple glow today. There was so little light that she couldn't even tell if smoke writhed on the ground or if Ria was nearby.

Cold swept across the back of her neck, making her shiver.

"Ashra," Narra called out quietly. She squinted into the dark, but saw nothing more than the faintest of glows in the center of the room. "Ashra?"

"My Daughter," Ashra's voice purred around her on all sides. "It's been awhile."

Narra winced. "Apologies. The war has been holding my attention."

"I see," Ashra said. Her voice had gone as cold as the cellar air.

"I need your help," Narra said. "I know you said you wouldn't be involved with the empire anymore, but Marina has retaken the Imperial Palace. We need to take it back, but with the war going on at the border, we can hardly remove soldiers just to regain control of the palace."

Ashra's laugh reverberated in her ears until Narra clapped her hands over them to stop the ringing filling her head. When the sound died off, she lowered her hands again.

"I've already been involved enough as is," Ashra said. The glow in the cellar strengthened until Narra could see Ashra seated on her black throne, her cheek lying in the palm of her hand. "You need to learn to solve your own problems. What kind of mother would I be if I just did everything for you?"

Heat flared through Narra's chest. *You're not my mother.*

Ashra's eyes widened slightly before they burned with fury. Suddenly, Ashra wasn't sitting on her throne, but standing directly in front of Narra. "What did you say, Daughter?"

Narra blanched. The thought had been as unexpected to her as it was to Lady Death. She barely even considered Khlara to be her mother.

Ashra narrowed her eyes and growled. "I don't think you quite understand how this works, Daughter. You are *mine*. I command *you*. You are my daughter. I am your mother. You will do as I say, or you will die."

Narra's heart pounded hard and her fingers trembled as she stared into the dark, bottomless eyes of death. She nodded slowly, her mind stuttering to come up with something to say.

Lady Death smiled humorlessly and gripped Narra's

chin. She wrenched it up hard so Narra was forced to stare into Ashra's eyes. "I have a mission for you, Daughter."

"A mission?" Narra asked. She inhaled deeply through her nose, trying to return to her sensible mind. "I can't. I'm busy with—"

"What did I *just say*?"

Narra slammed her teeth together with an audible click. *Obey or die.*

"Exactly." Ashra caressed Narra's cheek with the back of her fingers. "My mission for you, my Daughter, is to find and kill Khlara Rheka."

Narra's eyes widened and her heart stopped. She blinked stupidly at the goddess, her mind struggling to catch up. Ashra wanted Narra to kill her own mother?

Her heart started back up too hard, squeezing painfully in her chest. She struggled to breathe and to find a way out of this. Ashra's words echoed in her mind. *You will do as I say, or you will die.*

"I'm glad you understand." Ashra released Narra's chin. "There will be only one mother in your life, and it won't be that wretched woman."

Narra opened her mouth to speak—to protest the murder of her own kin—but no words would come. Ashra smirked and took a step back before reaching into the blackness of her dress. When she pulled her hand back out, she held a long dagger that seemed to be crafted by some kind of ivory. The blade was sharp and pointed and white in color. The top of the hilt looked like two skeleton hands clutching the blade. The rest of the hilt was a larger bone of some kind, like one in a person's leg.

"You will kill your mother with this." Ashra displayed the dagger on both of her palms and nodded at it, motioning for Narra to take it.

Narra hesitated for only a moment before clutching the bone dagger and lifting it up to inspect the blade in the low light. "What is it?" Narra whispered.

Ashra smiled. "That isn't important. Just know that you must kill Khlara with this weapon. It will absorb her life essence and prove the deed is done."

Narra gulped. She didn't know what to say. She didn't know what to do to convince the goddess that she didn't want to do this—couldn't do this. She might have sent the Talcotta assassins after Khlara like a pack of wild dogs, but Khlara had time to run. The woman had escaped. And now Ashra wanted her to track down the woman who gave birth to her? Narra didn't even know where to start.

"I'm sure you'll come up with something." Ashra chuckled darkly and spun around. She returned to her throne with a theatrical swoosh of her black skirts. Once she was seated, she tilted her chin up at Narra. "You may go."

Narra fell back a step, then another. Her entire body felt like lead. Her bones were steel and her skin was iron. She slowly turned around and made her way up the steps into the night air.

Even as the cold licked her skin, heat engulfed her. Lady Death had asked for some unbelievable things in the past, but this was too far. She couldn't do this.

"How'd it go?" Mika asked.

Narra looked up. She'd forgotten he was there. The second he saw her face, his eyebrows furrowed and his smile dropped. He pushed off the wall he'd been leaning against and crossed the yard.

"Are you all right?" He stopped in front of her and quickly inspected her.

"Yeah," she said, her voice barely above a whisper. "Let's go."

Before Mika could mutter another word, she slipped by him and launched herself back over the fence. Even as her feet hit the sidewalk, that weight continued to lie on her like a heavy stone.

What in Srah's name was she supposed to do now?

Narra stepped into her apartment building, shivering from the cold air outside. She rubbed her arms as she walked to the staircase on the far side of the small lobby and began the climb to the third floor. Mika followed quietly. They'd hardly spoken a word since they'd left Ashra's cellar. She wasn't ready to talk about what the Goddess of Death had just asked her to do. Even if she was, Mika was the last person she'd tell.

They reached the third floor in total silence. She slipped into the familiar hall with gas lamps drawn low. Only faint light lit their way up to the vault-like door that barred her way home.

Mika snorted as Narra stopped in front of her door. She narrowed her eyes at the assassin, who looked all too amused all of a sudden.

"This suits you," Mika said.

Narra ignored him and began unlocking the door, one

lock at a time. By the time she flung the door open, her annoyance had faded, and cold dread replaced it once more. She had failed her mission. She should have known that Ashra wouldn't help them after all she'd done. But she didn't expect her to do *this*.

"She's home!" Erik called down the hallway. He flashed a grin from the kitchen doorway, then waved her in.

Narra sighed as she followed her best friend into the kitchen. Asher and Therin sat at the small table, their large frames dwarfing the furniture. They held half empty mugs of tea.

"You're back," Asher said. His eyes were wide and hopeful.

Narra looked at Erik, her eyebrows furrowing. His answering look of understanding calmed some of the dread in her, but it didn't push it away entirely.

"I am," Narra said.

The door to the small bathing room and the door to Narra's room opened simultaneously. Avalon peeked out of Narra's bedroom while Dom stepped out of the bathing room. His cheeks were pink like he'd just washed his face, and Avalon quickly trotted over.

The moment the pirate saw the look on Narra's face, she took the thief's hand in hers and squeezed. "There will be another way."

Narra nodded before turning back to face those in the kitchen. "They won't help."

Asher's face fell. He stared into the steam rising from his tea. "We need to head back to the warfront, then." He raised his gaze to peer at Therin. "We'll head to my home in East

Gardens. I have a steamwagon we can use to return to Bordertown."

"Yes, sir," Therin said. He sat up straighter, looking like he wanted to salute and clap his heels together.

Erik continued to eye her from across the room. He knew there was something she wasn't saying, but he wouldn't pry in front of everyone.

"Ah, it seems your shadow has returned as well," Dom said.

Narra glanced over her shoulder to find Dom raising an eyebrow at Mika, whose smirk was firmly back in place. "He never left, unfortunately."

"You act as if you don't *adore* my presence." Mika's grin widened to flash his teeth.

"I don't," she said in a Clint-like monotone.

Mika mock gasped and held a hand over his chest.

Before he could continue with his theatrics, Asher and Therin stood, the legs of their chairs scraping over the worn wood floor.

"We should head out now," Asher said, all business.

Narra nodded. "Let's go." She stepped out of the doorway to allow Asher and Therin through. The general led the way out of her apartment while Narra and Erik brought up the rear. Before she could turn to lock the door, Erik was already on it.

He shot her a small smile over his shoulder. "Everything will be okay now that we're back together again."

Narra couldn't help the twitch of her lips. He was right in a way. If these were normal circumstances, their reunion would mean the end of their enemies. But there was nothing normal about the last few days. Rova was at war. Ashra wanted Narra to kill her mother. Marina had taken back the Imperial Palace, and they were about to lead a siege against the former empress.

Nothing about this was normal.

Narra sighed. She wrapped an arm around him, pulling him into a quick, awkward hug. When she let go and stepped away, Erik gave her a questioning look, but she only shook her head. She'd tell him everything later. But first they had to deal with Marina and the palace. Then she could think about Ashra's demands.

"Come on," Narra said.

As she turned on her heel and descended the stairs back out of her apartment building, she was all too aware of Mika's gaze penetrating the side of her head. He knew something was up, but the assassin stalking her every move was another problem for later.

"HOW ARE seven people supposed to fit in one steamwagon?" Avalon asked as she walked a circle around the large vehicle. She pursed her lips and narrowed her eyes suspiciously, like it was the steamwagon's fault they all couldn't fit.

Asher looked at the pirate. "Seven of us made it here in one, didn't we?"

"Yes, but that was with Narra laid across three laps," Avalon said, still staring at the steamwagon.

Narra's cheeks heated at the memory. She'd been avoiding thinking about it since.

"I guess I could take one for the team," Avalon continued on a sigh. "It's only fair since you did last time." Her gaze met Narra's, resignation settled there.

"No," Narra said immediately. A swell of protective energy filled her. She didn't want Avalon sitting in anyone's lap. Avalon was *hers*. Narra froze, her eyes widening and her lips parting as she realized what she'd just thought. She'd claimed Avalon as her own. Even if it was only in her head, her face reddened.

Avalon laughed. "It's okay. I don't mind."

Narra shook her head mutely. *No way*.

"That's all right, the little death bringer can sit in my lap anytime," Mika said. He wiggled his eyebrows in Narra's direction, making her groan.

Erik slapped Mika's arm and glared at the assassin. Mika blinked in surprise before returning Erik's annoyed look.

Asher sighed. "Enough. We're all adults here." He pushed between the glaring thief and assassin to get in the front seat. Once he'd slammed the door shut, he stared at them all pointedly until Therin and Dom sprung into action.

Dom, the gentleman that he was, guided Avalon around to the other side of the front cabin. He opened the door and helped her inside before climbing in after her. That left Narra with Erik, Mika, and Therin in the backseat. She bit her tongue on another groan. She was definitely not sitting on Mika's or Therin's lap. She'd rather pluck out her own eyeballs.

That left Erik. Her embarrassment faded slightly, and her pounding heart began to calm. At least Erik was her safe place.

Erik opened the door behind the driver's seat and quickly climbed in. He stayed in the seat instead of shifting to the middle, forcing Mika and Therin to go around to the other side and decide who was going to be squished in the middle.

While they bickered on the other side of the steamwagon, Erik helped her climb up onto his lap before closing the door behind her. Once it was closed, she leaned back against the door and wiggled to adjust herself. When she was finally mostly comfortable, even with Erik's bony knees sticking into her backside, she stilled.

"Are you two coming or what?" Narra called out to Mika and Therin, who had yet to climb inside. Upon seeing her raised eyebrows, Mika hopped in first and scooted right into the middle until her knees were pressed against his. She narrowed her eyes as he grinned.

Therin cursed under his breath and climbed in last.

Once they were all settled with the doors firmly shut, Asher let out a heavy sigh. "Are we ready to go then? Time *is* of the essence."

"Ready," Narra said quickly. She wanted no more wasted time.

"Thank Srah," Asher hissed under his breath. He started up the engine, which Narra realized he'd already been stoking for some time. Heat filled the vehicle, chasing away the cold of outside.

The steamwagon rumbled beneath them, and then they were on the road.

~

THE SUN WAS PEEKING over the horizon by the time they arrived at the warfront. Narra could barely feel her backside, let alone her legs. Most of her had gone numb from being jostled all night, and she yawned lazily. They were about to have a long day, and she hoped she'd be able to sleep on the return trip to Rova City, or else she'd be in no shape to engage in battle.

The steamwagon rolled to a stop at the edge of camp, and Asher glanced over his shoulder in warning. Narra slipped on her hood, as did Erik, Avalon, and Mika. They all stumbled out of the vehicle, lacking the grace Narra had come to associate with their professions.

"*Ancestors*," she cursed as she leaned against the steamwagon's side. It took almost a full minute for her legs to stop feeling like pins and needles were stabbing every inch of them. When feeling returned, she sighed in relief and stretched.

"Follow me," Asher said gruffly. He barely waited for them to assemble and trail after him before he began marching through the camp. He nodded a greeting to many of his men, who looked happy to see him return. They gave the rest of his party curious glances but said nothing while their general was in their midst.

They reached the center of camp, and Asher threw open the flaps of the war tent.

"General!" Gabriel gasped. He held a hand to his chest as he caught his breath. The others looked equally as startled. "You've returned! Thank Srah!"

Asher grunted a greeting as the rest of them filed in behind him. As soon as Narra stepped inside, silence descended in the tent. Gabriel, Sarin, and Lasar stared at her like they were witnessing the rise of the dead.

"You're alive." Gabriel was the first to regain some semblance of self. He cleared his throat several times and his forehead wrinkled. "How?"

Sarin scanned Narra from head to toe, her eyes narrowed in suspicion. "How indeed."

"I'm not so easy to kill," Narra said. She tilted her chin up.

"What has happened in my absence?" Asher said, taking control of his war tent.

Everyone gathered around the large table at the center of the tent. Narra skirted around the edge to put her back to her usual exit at the hall between tents. Avalon, Erik, and Mika followed, standing at her side while she leaned over to assess the movements of war.

True to her word, Danicka didn't seem to have attacked in their absence. The silver wolves and iron lions all remained in the same positions upon the map. The lions guarded Bordertown while the wolves pushed them back farther and farther into their own country.

"Nothing, sire," Gabriel said. He stood tall as he addressed his general. "There have been no attacks. We've kept an eye on the battlefield, but there hasn't been so much as a scout issued beyond the wall."

Asher nodded appreciatively. "Excellent. At least Empress Danicka has remained true to her word."

"Indeed," Gabriel said.

"But that is all about to end," Narra said. "The two days are almost up."

Asher looked up at her. His gaze was dark with worry. He

had realized the same thing. "It is." He sighed and looked at Gabriel, Sarin, and Lasar. "There is something I need to apprise you of. I'm sure you heard from the messenger that Marina escaped custody."

Gabriel, Sarin, and Lasar nodded gravely.

"Well, it's much worse than that." Asher straightened, his jaw set. "She's retaken the Imperial Palace."

Sarin gasped. "What?"

"That's impossible!" Lasar snapped.

"How can this be?" Gabriel asked.

Asher shook his head. "I don't know. But the Palace Guard have been wiped out or imprisoned by now, I'm sure. We barely escaped with our lives." He sent a grateful look Narra's way, making her skin heat.

"What are we going to do?" Gabriel asked gruffly. "We can't spare the manpower to send more than a platoon back to Rova City."

"I know," Asher said. "But with the support from West Port still a couple of days away, we have to do *something*."

"Of course, sire," Sarin said. "But General Gabriel is right. If the war is about to restart, we can't spare many to return to Rova City, even for such a just cause."

Narra looked between the military men and woman. Her heart began to race as she tried to come up with a solution for them. All of Rova City's military was on the war front between Rova and Kiznaiver. While they had support on the way, they didn't have time to wait for it.

What manner of chaos could Marina cause while she sat on the throne of Rova? What would she do to their capitol city while the rest of them were at war?

Narra ground her teeth and stared at the map. Rova City was large, sitting at the edge of the map with great black walls surrounding. At the top of the city was a castle with spires that pierced the sky. Marina was taking over that city right now. She was in that castle, on that throne.

Anger flashed through her. Narra barely heard the arguing around her as her mind flew in all directions—desperate for an answer to their problem.

Danicka had given them two days of reprieve from the war. She was true to her word—an honorable woman. Could Narra convince her to extend the reprieve? If they had a few extra days, they could return to Rova City and put Marina to rest for good. Once that was dealt with, they could return to war.

Her heart pounded hard as she looked up to assess the faces around her. Gabriel's was red with anger, and Sarin's was impassive as usual. Asher's eyebrow twitched—he was having a hard time holding onto his civility.

Narra took a step away from the table. They were so engrossed in conversation that no one looked her way. She turned to Erik and leaned over to speak in his ear. "Watch Avalon for me," she said.

Erik shot her a surprised look as she leaned back. He opened his mouth to argue, but she quickly shook her head. This wasn't the time. She had to go *now* before the enemy camp was fully awake.

"You don't think she can handle herself?" Erik asked. He raised an eyebrow as he shot a glance at Avalon, who was as engrossed in the argument as anyone else in the room.

Narra smiled. "I know she can, but I can't handle losing her."

Erik's wrinkled forehead softened and he nodded in understanding. He watched Narra as she slipped away from the others and into the canvas hallway at the back of the tent.

With the others out of sight, Narra dove out of the tent, her heart racing as she tore across camp for the woods.

Narra slipped across the short gap between the camp and the forest, her breath puffing around her in clouds. The sun was still barely over the horizon, sending long rays of orange over the tops of the tents. The valley might look pretty if it weren't for the war tents and the makeshift wall on the horizon.

"Where are we heading?"

Narra jumped at Mika's voice and spun to glare at him. "Would you stop following me?"

Mika flashed a grin. "You know the deal, sweetheart."

"We have no deal," Narra growled. She turned and stormed into the woods, heading to the Kiznaiver camp.

"Not per se," Mika said thoughtfully. His footsteps were silent behind her, only aggravating her further. "But I'd like to think of it as a silent contract. I could simply pluck you from your adventures and tie you up in a cellar somewhere until mother dearest comes looking for you."

Narra shot him a glare over her shoulder. "I would kill you before you slipped the shackles on my wrists."

Mika chuckled. "Maybe."

Narra stopped and spun to face him.

He stopped abruptly, his boots crushing the leaves beneath him. He scowled at the small sound and glared at his feet.

"Let's get this straight, shall we? I allow *you* to accompany me. I allow *you* to be in my presence and follow my friends and me. I *allow you* to be here. Do not be mistaken, assassin. You are here because I'm allowing it, not the other way around."

Mika's smirk dropped and darkness flashed in his gaze. "Don't test me, little death bringer."

Narra took a step closer as angry heat flared through her chest. "No. Do not test *me*, assassin."

He narrowed his eyes at her, mimicking her angry look. They remained like that for several long moments, staring each other down. Narra could see the fury in his gaze, and the frustration at having to deal with her. He didn't seem like a man who was used to strong women. Sure, he enjoyed her cutting tongue and her stubborn attitude—he might even like that she had bested him not once, but twice—but she knew he would kill her once his contract was over. This was no friendship. They tolerated one another. But if he kept testing her, he'd soon realize what it meant to be a Commander of the Thieves Guild.

A branch snapped nearby, forcing them to break apart. Narra leapt back, a dagger already in hand, while Mika did the same in the opposite direction. She scanned the forest, her heartbeat speeding up as she looked between tall pine trees nestled into the thick undergrowth.

Her breathing calmed when the crunch of leaves sounded farther away. Whoever was nearby, they weren't heading towards her and Mika.

Narra sighed and spun on her heel. She was tired of this. She was wasting time. "Hurry up," she snapped. She stormed through the trees, keeping as silent as the grave as she worked her way through the forest to the Kiznaiver camp.

The second it came into view between the trees, Mika grabbed her elbow. "Death bringer, you're not doing what I think you're doing."

Narra yanked her elbow from his grip. "I'm going to convince the empress to give us more time." Before she could march forward, Mika stilled her with a look.

"You're playing with fire, Rheka."

Narra almost winced. It was the first time Mika had called her anything but death bringer. It didn't sound right coming from him. "I'm only doing what I have to."

"And you have to get yourself killed?" he snapped.

"Why is it you men think I'm so easy to kill?" She raised an eyebrow. "You've seen me survive a gunshot wound. I won't be killed by Danicka."

Mika sighed. "You only survived that wound because of your friend."

"Ria," Narra said.

"Ria," Mika said. "You only survived because of Ria and her magic. If you are wounded way up north like this again, what are the chances you'll survive?"

Narra tilted her chin up. "I'm not planning on being shot a second time."

Mika growled. "It doesn't have to be a gunshot. What if the empress cuts you too deep to heal with that whip of hers?"

"She won't."

"She almost did last time."

"I would have won that fight." Narra narrowed her eyes.

"I know," Mika said. He faltered slightly and avoided her gaze. "But she almost matched you."

"Almost," Narra agreed. "But almost doesn't win a fight."

Mika's lips quirked. "It can if you aren't smart enough to run."

Narra scoffed. "This conversation is pointless."

Mika hummed his agreement.

Before Mika could pull her into more conversation, Narra slipped through the forest to the tree line. She crouched as she worked her way along the border. She didn't have the darkness of night to hide in, so she'd have to be even more careful than usual.

She scanned the tents, the trees, and the perimeter of the camp. The patrol had passed by recently but now had their backs to the trees as they walked around the edge of camp closest to the battlefield.

Her heart raced as she braced herself to run. There was no one at this edge of camp—not right now at least. She could be across the space between the first tent and the trees in only a few bounds.

Narra took a fortifying breath. "Let's go."

She dove from the trees and raced across the open strip

of land. It felt like minutes had passed before she was diving between tents, though it could have only been a few seconds. As soon as she was huddled between tents, she breathed easier. She crouched low and strained her ears to listen for signs of pursuit.

"You're clear," Mika rumbled. He crouched next to her, a bored look on his face.

Narra took one last look around before she began winding through tents toward the center of camp. She passed men and women who were cooking breakfast, strapping on their armor, or sharing a quick laugh by the fire.

She lurked in what remained of the shadows and silently slipped through camp until she was crouching behind a familiar wall of boxes and chicken cages. The chickens squawked at the unknown presence and tilted their heads at Narra and Mika.

"Hush," Narra hissed quietly at the birds. She kneeled by the tent flap she'd previously cut open to find the stitching still broken. Perfect. No one would expect a thing.

The rumble of men's voices echoed inside, along with the cut of a woman's irritated voice. She recognized Danicka, but none of the others.

"Enough of this reprieve, Your Majesty," a man growled. "We should attack while they don't expect it."

"You seek to dishonor me?" Danicka snapped. "No. I promised the Rovans two days of respite. I will not deny them that."

"All of this for some girl?" a man with a high voice asked.

Danicka sighed. "It isn't just for *some girl*. It's because one of my men dishonored us all. He took the fight upon himself. He took *my duel* from me. He probably killed her."

Narra's eyebrows furrowed. The empress actually sounded sorry about that. But why?

"I understand, Your Majesty," another man said. His voice was vaguely familiar. Maybe he was the one who had been speaking to the empress in her tent the last time Narra was eavesdropping. "It is only one more day."

"One more day could mean the reinforcements they've most likely already sent for will join them on the field tomorrow!" The first man with the deepest voice was nearly shouting at the others.

"Then we will face them!" Danicka shot back. "And we *will* win."

"Her majesty is right," the familiar man said. "The Rovans will fall."

Grumbles of agreement filled the tent.

"Now, let's meet back tonight," Danicka said. "We can talk strategy then."

Several voices murmured goodbyes before footsteps told Narra they had left. Once silence had descended for several long moments, she ducked her head in to see if the room was empty.

Danicka sat in the largest seat at the war council table. She had one leg crossed over the other and was sipping idly on a goblet. Her gaze was distant as she stared at the table. Though Narra could only see part of her profile from this angle, Danicka looked exhausted.

Narra ducked her head back outside and exchanged a glance with Mika.

"Well?" he whispered.

"She's alone," Narra said. "I'm going in."

"Then so am I."

Narra didn't bother arguing with the assassin. She eased the flaps of the tent open and carefully slipped inside. A cart was pushed up near her entrance, obscuring her from sight. As soon as her entire body was inside, she stood.

She didn't want to raise an alarm, but she did want to speak with Danicka one on one. She wasn't there to hurt the empress, or threaten her, but she would if she had to. Rova needed this reprieve. They needed more time.

"Good morning," Narra said.

Danicka jumped and dropped her goblet, spilling wine across the table. The empress was on her feet before Narra could blink. Her fingers clasped the hilt of her dagger and her eyes widened in recognition. "You." She paused and scanned Narra from head to toe. Shock registered on her face. "You're alive."

"I am." Narra took a step into the room, allowing Mika to slip in behind her.

As he straightened to his full height, Danicka glanced at the assassin warily and drew her blade.

"I'm not here to harm you."

Danicka gave Narra a look of disbelief before her gaze returned to Mika. "Then why have you brought a Talcotta assassin?"

Narra raised her eyebrows. How had Danicka picked him out so easily? Narra hadn't known what he was until she saw his sword.

Mika looked equally surprised, though he quickly hid it

with a smirk. "Your Majesty." He tipped his head in a greeting.

"He follows me," Narra said blandly. "It has nothing to do with you."

Danicka's wrinkled forehead didn't smooth. She continued to regard them both with open suspicion, but she didn't call for help. It would have been the smartest thing to do, but Narra had a feeling that Danicka wasn't scared of many people.

As the empress tilted her head, the crown of bones and steel that sat upon her head reflected the light of the gas lamps. It was a good reminder to Narra that Danicka held far more power than she might realize. Whether spirit magic was the same as the magic Ashra held, or even the magic the other Daughters held, Narra couldn't be sure, but it seemed like it was strong enough to embolden the empress.

"If you say so," Danicka said. Her blue eyes flashed with curiosity. "How are you alive?"

Narra frowned. "I'm not easy to kill."

Danicka raised a brow. "Do you have magic as well?"

Narra's scowl deepened. She said nothing to confirm or deny Danicka's suspicion. Instead, she took another step into the room. "We have unfinished business."

"You speak of our duel?" Danicka asked, raising a white eyebrow.

Narra nodded. It was the only way she could think of to sway the empress. If Danicka wouldn't agree to extend their reprieve, she would hold the duel over her head.

"What is it you want..." the empress trailed off, waiting for a name.

"Rheka," Narra said.

Danicka's lips curved in a sly smile. "What is it you want, Rheka?"

"I want you to extend the reprieve you gave us."

Danicka's eyebrows shot up. "Excuse me?"

"You heard me." Narra narrowed her eyes.

Danicka frowned. "You're mad! I've already given you two days." Her eyes scanned Narra from head to toe. "And here you are, alive. I should lift the reprieve today."

Narra took a step forward, a growl rising in her throat.

"There are matters involving the empire that are beyond your understanding."

"Oh?" Danicka inclined her head. "Then why don't you explain them?"

Narra inhaled deeply, trying to rein in the fire in her chest. "I can't without the permission of my emperor."

"How disappointing."

"All I ask is for an extension. A week. Give us one week to deal with matters in our own empire so we can come back and fight evenly against yours." Narra's heart pounded hard. She hoped desperately that the empress would agree. They *needed* this time. Without it, the empire could fall.

"You expect me to give you *a week*? You're insane." Danicka shook her head. "A week would allow the reinforcements I'm sure you've called to arrive. A week could allow you time to enlist hundreds of new recruits. A week is impossible. I won't agree to it."

Narra bit the inside of her cheek to keep from groaning. She was so beyond frustrated, but lucky for her, she had an ace up her sleeve. "Fine. Let's duel for it."

Danicka's eyes widened in surprise. "Duel for it?"

"Yes." Narra let a smirk pull up the corners of her lips. Such an honorbound woman could hardly refuse to finish their duel. From the glare Danicka gave her, she knew it too.

"Unbelievable," Danicka growled. Her fists clenched and trembled with rage. "You'd really use that against me."

Narra tilted up her chin. "I'll do whatever I must to save my empire."

Danicka scoffed. "Your empire isn't worth saving."

"Says the one about to lose."

Mika chuckled behind her, but Narra didn't dare look back to see what was so funny.

"Let's make a deal," Narra said. "If *I* win, you will help me by increasing Rova's reprieve by one week." Danicka flinched. "If *you* win, you can appease your generals and go back to fighting us today."

Danicka narrowed her eyes suspiciously. "You've been spying on me?"

Narra shrugged.

Danicka sheathed her dagger. Her fingers itched at her side like she wanted to strangle Narra.

"All right," Danicka said through gritted teeth. "I accept your challenge, but I won't lose. Prepare to go to war, Rheka."

Narra simply smiled. She was born for this. Danicka had caught her off guard last time, but this time she was prepared. Narra knew the empress' moves. She knew how she fought. Danicka had hardly gotten a look at what Narra was capable of, and she was ready to show her.

"I'll prepare an area for us to fight," Danicka said. She took a step back to the flap of the tent. "I suggest you remain here until I'm finished."

"You wouldn't go tattling on us, now would you?" Mika asked.

Narra wanted to grab her dagger at the danger edging into his voice. Danicka narrowed her eyes, clearly not liking the threat.

"I would never dishonor myself like that," Danicka said, and then she left the tent.

"You're sure you can win?" Mika asked as the tent flap settled back into place.

Narra stepped away from the assassin and turned so she no longer had her back to him. "I'm sure."

"I hope so, or else you might just cost your friends the last day of their reprieve," Mika said. He sounded like he was teasing, but his eyes were serious.

"I'll cost them nothing," Narra said firmly.

Mika shrugged and said nothing more as they waited for the empress' return.

NARRA STOOD in a small clearing ringed by high tents. It was just outside the war tent at the center of the Kiznaiver camp, and it had enough coverage to keep them Danicka and her hidden from sight while they fought. She surveyed her surroundings, which were empty of soldiers. What had Danicka told them to make them leave?

Danicka stepped out of the largest tent in camp, directly across from the war tent. Four men accompanied her, all with equally pale skin and hair, though none had quite the white-blonde of the empress. Her blue eyes flashed ferociously as she walked around the edge of the small clearing to face off against Narra. The empress tilted her chin up and laid her hands on her hips.

"Are you ready?" Narra asked.

Mika backed away from the center of the clearing to stand at the edge. He eyed the four men following the empress. Two of them whispered quietly in Danicka's ear. The empress scoffed and nodded before motioning them away with a flick of her hand.

The youngest of the four narrowed his eyes suspiciously at Narra. He wore full Kiznaiver armor, metal and leather strapped to his body, and had two short swords on his hips. He had a stern look about him for someone who couldn't be much older than the empress.

"Yes," Danicka said, interrupting Narra's inspection of the Kiznai. "Are you ready to return to the battlefield today?"

Narra smiled. "No. But that won't matter when you yield to me."

Danicka's confidence wavered. She flicked a glance at the two oldest men in her small party. They exchanged a wary glance before nodding to the empress.

"This isn't a battle to the death, then?" Danicka asked.

Narra chuckled. She couldn't help it. "No. I wouldn't rob your people of your leadership, and I'm needed by far too many to let you kill me."

Danicka's eyebrow rose. "I agree to your terms."

Questions flashed through the empress' eyes, but she asked none of them. Instead, she took two steps into the clearing and removed her bladed whip from her belt.

Narra mimicked her actions so they stood equal distances into the clearing, leaving almost fifteen feet between them.

"Good luck, death bringer," Mika called to her.

Again, Danicka's men exchanged glances, but Danicka didn't remove her eyes from Narra.

The empress was a true warrior. She was confident, strong, and battle-hardened. Danicka wouldn't underestimate Narra a second time. She had to remember that.

Narra unclasped her cloak from her shoulders and let it fly into the wind. It flapped for only a few moments before Mika plucked it from the air. She didn't want the cloak hindering her movements. It was just something to grab onto, much like her hair. At least in a battle against another woman, Narra assumed Danicka wouldn't succumb to such a cheap tactic.

"Shall we begin on the count of three?" Danicka asked. Her voice was pitched low, an edge of danger to it, yet she shifted from foot to foot like she was anxious. Her white hair billowed around her, held back by the Crown of Bones atop her head.

Narra ignored the slight prickle of magic in her mind and nodded. "On three."

Danicka glanced at the youngest of her troop. "Count down for us."

The young man nodded. He took a single step forward, glancing between his empress and Narra with a look of worry in his eyes. When he caught Narra's eye, his gaze turned steely. "One. Two. Three. Engage!"

Danicka flicked her wrist and her whip *cracked* through the air. Narra had already jumped in anticipation of Danicka's impatience, and the whip slapped the ground where she'd just been standing.

The empress growled as she pulled back hard, but Narra was already rushing forward. She yanked her sword from its sheath and dove at Danicka.

A blinding cut of silver flashed through the air and Narra barely backpedalled in time to keep from getting another cut across her cheek. She breathed hard, her adrenaline rushing through her veins.

Danicka was possibly the best opponent Narra had ever

had. She relished fighting the empress again and hoped it wouldn't be the last time. A fight like this couldn't compare to training with anyone else.

"I nearly got you," Danicka said, most likely in an attempt to distract her.

Narra chuckled as she slipped free of another crack of the whip. She didn't bother responding. Instead, she watched the flick of Danicka's wrist. The movement was growing familiar. Each time she moved her hand and arm in a particular way, the whip arched in the same pattern, obeying its master's command.

The thief dodged crack after crack of the whip until Danicka scowled.

"Are you not going to attack me?" Danicka snapped. She flicked her wrist as she said it, but Narra had already leapt far away from her strike.

Narra smirked as she dodged, growing closer to the empress little by little. Danicka must have finally realized it because her eyes widened and her speed increased.

She whipped her entire arm through the air, bringing her whip in closer to attack Narra. But Narra knew that was exactly what Danicka would do. It was the same thing she'd done the last time Narra got too close.

She recalled their fight on the battlefield. Danicka had used her whip until Narra had gotten too close, and then she'd turned her whip into a blade. Though the empress was an accomplished sword fighter as well, nothing could compare to Narra's speed with a blade. All she needed to do was force Danicka to make the switch.

Narra leapt free of Danicka's next strike and charged forward.

The empress cursed as Narra got closer. She tried three more cracks of her whip before her eyebrows furrowed and she snapped her wrist in a new way. The whip went rigid, turning into a long straight blade. Each section of the once fluid weapon now as stiff as a board.

Narra grinned. Perfect. This is exactly what she wanted. She slammed her blade against Danicka's and pushed hard before quickly falling back a step and spinning to slice at Danicka's knee.

Danicka moved just in time to avoid the injury, thrusting her blade into the side of Narra's.

The thief spun again, slicing at the empress' hip and then again at her chest. Each time Danicka dodged or blocked, a growing look of tension built in the wrinkle of her forehead. Danicka ground her teeth as Narra clanged their blades together once again. They pushed apart, blades extended between each other.

The empress must have seen an opening because her eyes lit up, and then she grabbed the dagger from her hip.

Narra didn't allow Danicka time to use it. Instead, she crashed down on Danicka's blade with all of her strength.

Air burst from Danicka's lungs, bathing Narra's face in her hot breath. While the empress struggled to hold Narra's blade away from her throat, Narra grabbed the bony hilt of the dagger closest to her fingers.

She dove to the side suddenly, making Danicka fall forward with a yelp. The empress saved herself from hitting the ground, but by the time she spun around, Narra had her sword pointed at Danicka's abdomen and the bone dagger pointed at her head.

Danicka's eyes widened in shock, but before Narra could claim victory, her dagger began to vibrate in her hand, a soft hum permeating the air.

Narra's eyebrows furrowed, but she didn't dare glance at her weapon instead of the empress. Whatever was happening, she pushed it aside and smirked at Danicka.

"Yield," Narra commanded.

Danicka's wide eyes weren't trained on the thief anymore. Instead, she regarded Narra's dagger with something like awe sparking in her eyes.

Narra narrowed her eyes and her smile dropped. Danicka said nothing. With a growl of irritation, Narra pushed her dagger forward a few inches, pointing it at the crown of Danicka's head. The blade hummed harder, and that's when she realized the same thing was happening with Danicka's crown. She could just make out the slight tremor in the bones and steel.

"How did you get that?" Danicka asked on a whisper.

"*Yield*," Narra said more forcefully this time.

The awed glaze in Danicka's eyes faded as she blinked awake from whatever spell she was under. With a thousand questions running through her mind, she looked Narra in the eye.

Danicka smiled. "I yield."

"Come with me," Danicka insisted before Narra had even lowered her weapons.

Narra blinked in surprise as Danicka spooled her whip and returned her weapons to her belt. She glanced back at Danicka's generals, bodyguards, or whatever they were, but the four men looked equally as confused.

Danicka walked with purpose to the war tent, passing directly by the thief. Narra stood dumbfounded for only a moment longer before she slowly lowered and then holstered her weapons. She looked between the Kiznai and Mika, who looked startled as well. With a small shrug, Narra followed Danicka into the war tent.

The second she stepped under the flap, footsteps pounded behind her. Narra had barely taken a few steps around the large meeting table when the four Kiznai burst into the room. They followed their empress around the opposite side of the table, giving Narra dirty looks as they went.

Mika slipped in after them and came to Narra's side, not bothering to hide the fact his fingers were wrapped around his dagger. He passed Narra her cloak without a word, and she thanked him. She clipped it to her shoulders before turning her attention to the empress.

Danicka paced behind the largest seat at the table, her forehead wrinkled in concentration. "Do you have any idea how rare it is to find an object like that?"

Narra glanced down at the bone dagger tucked into her belt. "No," she said carefully.

Danicka stopped pacing and looked at Narra like she was stupid. "How can you not know? You must have constructed it from the ancient bones of a spirit god just as I did."

Narra's eyes widened. "What?"

The empress scanned Narra's face before her shoulders slumped. "You really didn't, did you?"

Narra shook her head, still too shocked to say anything.

"That's unfortunate. I was hoping to have someone to share this with."

Narra's gazed flicked up to Danicka's crown. "Your crown."

Danicka chuckled darkly. "The Crown of Bones. Made with permission from a Spirit God of Nature after he was used and corrupted by our former High Priest."

Narra didn't have the words. What was this girl talking about? She knew that the crown was where Danicka's magic came from; she could sense it every time the empress was near. But she had no idea what this magic meant or how it worked.

"Who does the dagger belong to? Where did you get it?" Danicka demanded, taking a step forward.

Narra instinctually took a step back. "I can't tell you that."

She might not be in Ashra's good graces at the moment, but she certainly wasn't going to explain that to Danicka.

Danicka's eyebrows furrowed. "You must."

Narra scoffed. "I *mustn't* do anything. You lost our duel. *You* must give us our reprieve and let us be on our way."

Danicka's jaw clenched. "I need to know more about your dagger."

"And I need to get back to my people."

Fury like blue fire flashed through Danicka's gaze. She spun on her heel and started pacing again. Her hair bobbed around her shoulders and back like it was possessed by storm winds. Her face grew unreadable as she walked briskly back and forth.

"Your Majesty," the youngest man interrupted. "What are you thinking? Shall we take the woman prisoner?"

Narra stiffened at the same time Danicka halted.

"Of course not," Danicka said. "That would be unsportsmanlike."

"Then you really intend to give the Rovans a week long reprieve?" one of the older men asked gruffly.

"That was the deal, was it not?" Danicka met Narra's gaze and waited until Narra nodded. "Yes, I will grant them their reprieve."

Narra's shoulders relaxed. She hadn't been worried about Danicka's word—the woman seemed *far* too keen on retaining her honor—but she'd been worried one of the men might push the empress into breaking it. She had no idea who they were or what positions they held. For all she knew, one of them could be Danicka's husband. Narra wasn't well apprised of Kiznaiver politics and news.

"Your Majesty!" the second older man gasped.

"Enough!" Danicka glared at her four comrades. When they said nothing, she returned her attention to Narra. "You truly won't give me any more information about your dagger?"

Narra shook her head.

Danicka's nostrils flared in annoyance before she cupped her hips with her hands. "Fine. Then I'm coming with you."

"What?" Mika gasped.

"You want to come with us? To our camp?" Narra asked. Her heart raced with uncertainty and confusion. What was this woman's game?

"Yes," Danicka said. "It is of the utmost importance that I gain more information about that dagger."

"You want to strike a deal," Narra realized aloud.

Danicka nodded. "Yes. Whatever you want this reprieve for, it has to be bad. You'll need my help."

Narra scoffed. "And what do you want in return?"

Danicka smiled. "I want you to tell me about your dagger. That's all."

Narra's eyebrows furrowed. She couldn't be serious. Danicka was the empress of a nation. She could hardly up and leave her people in the middle of a war just to follow Narra around.

"Your Majesty! You can't do this!" one of the older men

said.

Danicka didn't even glance at him. "Silence, Bernard. I am your empress. Don't think to tell me what to do."

Bernard stiffened. "Apologies, Your Majesty. I meant no harm by it."

This time Danicka did look at her soldier. "I know. Thank you for your concern, but as you know, I can handle myself."

"This seems too far-fetched," Narra said. "How do we know you won't try to harm our emperor, or attack us in our beds? We can't trust you."

Danicka looked at her in disbelief. "I would never do such a thing."

"I don't *know you*. How can I trust your word?" Narra narrowed her eyes.

Danicka mimicked Narra's glare. "I haven't had you imprisoned since you arrived, have I?" She raised her eyebrows meaningfully. "You must have realized by now that I would never dishonor myself or my people. I swear to you, Rheka, that I will not harm any of your people unless they move to harm me."

Narra worked her jaw back and forth. What a nuisance this woman was becoming. "I can't guarantee your safety."

The youngest of the four men stepped forward again, his green eyes flashing angrily. "You won't need to. I'll be accompanying Empress Danicka."

Danicka's gaze softened. "Mason, you really don't have to. You know I can take care of myself."

Mason shook his head. "As your personal bodyguard, I can't allow it. If you insist on going with these... people, then I'll be with you."

Danicka shook her head.

"I can't guarantee the safety of one of you, let alone two," Narra said dryly. She didn't know what Danicka expected. Narra wasn't the emperor. She had no say. But the more she thought about it, the more her heart pounded.

Narra was about to return to Rova City with only seven days to take the palace, execute Marina, and return to the battlefield—all while somehow staying alive. Danicka did seem true to her word thus far. She was honorable in all things, and Narra doubted that would change. It seemed like something ingrained in the empress' personality. Were all Kiznai people like this?

Danicka turned back to face Narra. "I know you can't guarantee our safety, but I know you will do your best." A knowing look passed through her eyes, making Narra wonder if Danicka could read her mind like Ashra.

"You'd really leave your people amidst an ongoing war?" Narra asked.

Danicka smiled. "It won't be ongoing for seven days, now will it?"

Narra sighed. From the determined look in Danicka's eyes, she wasn't going to back down. Narra almost told her everything just to keep her from coming—all about the dagger Ashra had given her and the mission the Goddess of Death had sent her on. But now that the idea of Danicka coming to Rova City was seeded in her mind, she could see all the benefits. The woman fought like no one else. She could help the Rovans just as much as Narra could. Together, they would be unstoppable.

"All right," Narra said. "If you agree to extend our reprieve, then I will allow you to come on two conditions."

Danicka raised an eyebrow. "And what are those?"

"You agree to use nothing you learn about us to your advantage in this war," Narra said, ignoring the scoffs of the men behind the empress.

"And?"

"You sit down with Asher Grayson, our next emperor, and hear what he has to say," Narra said. She tilted her chin up. She would not budge on these terms. If she could get Danicka to agree to a sit down with Asher, they might be able to end the war peacefully.

No matter how unlikely it was that the war would end with no more bloodshed, she had to try. Whether they could come to terms or not, remained to be seen, but it was worth the effort.

Danicka smiled and nodded. "I agree to your terms."

NARRA SLIPPED through the trees alongside Mika, heading back towards the Rovan camp. Before they'd departed, Danicka had taken a few moments to gather a cloak and a bag of her things. Her bodyguard, Mason, had done the same.

She'd heard every order Danicka had given before they'd departed, leaving no private time for the empress to deliver separate orders with Narra out of earshot. True to her word, Danicka had given the order to stall the war for seven days, but if she didn't return in that time, the Kiznai had been instructed to launch a full-scale attack on Rova's forces.

The empress had met Narra's eyes when she'd said it. Danicka had wanted her to know it was both a warning to Danicka's people and a threat to Narra's. If Narra didn't help bring the empress back in one piece by the end of the week, Narra's people would pay for it.

They spoke in hushed whispers, keeping several feet back from Narra and Mika.

Narra sighed, fogging the air in front of her. It was nearly noon, but the sky was dark and overcast. There was no movement on the battlefield, and only a few sentries monitored from the top of the makeshift wall.

As they grew closer and closer to camp, her heart began to pound. What had she done? She was bringing the enemy into their camp. Though Danicka had agreed not to act on anything she learned while with the Rovans, Narra had no way of knowing if the empress would keep her word.

Danicka might have been forthright and honest so far, but Narra was sure her honor could be stretched—especially when it came to her country.

"You did a foolish thing, death bringer," Mika whispered at her shoulder.

Narra sighed once more. "I know."

Mika didn't chuckle like she expected. Instead, when she looked at him, his face was grave. He didn't like this any more than she did.

"It will be fine," she said, more to assure herself than him.

What would Asher say when she brought Empress Danicka into their war tent? What would he say when she told him what she had won them? She was sure he'd be grateful for the extra time, but not so much for Danicka's presence.

Narra glanced over her shoulder, keeping an eye on their Kiznai companions.

Danicka met her gaze with blue steel. She didn't smile or look away. Her crown was missing, letting her hair fall on either side of her angular face. She looked less intimidating without it, maybe even a little innocent. The empress was only twenty-two, yet she had the battle prowess of a seasoned warrior.

Narra had to respect that, especially when the woman was running an empire too.

She looked away as shouts from camp met her ears. Laughter erupted somewhere at the edge of camp, making her brows furrow. They sounded drunk. Maybe it was their way of coping with the battle they expected tomorrow.

Narra slipped to the edge of the trees and crouched behind a thick trunk as she waited for the patrol to pass. Once they'd disappeared, she spied the perfect entrance and leapt from between the trees.

Footsteps pounded behind her as she raced across the short distance from the tree line to camp. She only slowed once she was safely between several unoccupied tents, the scent of coal drifting up her nose.

"Move with me, and stay quiet," Narra instructed. She made sure to receive a nod from Danicka and Mason before she turned and began making her way through camp.

True to their word, they did exactly what she said. After several minutes of ducking and running, the four of them crouched behind the crates next to the war tent. As usual, she checked the flap she'd ripped when they had first arrived. It remained broken.

"All right, we're going to go inside. Stay behind me, and let me explain what happened before you say anything," Narra said.

"Of course," Danicka said.

Narra waited for a brisk nod from Mason before turning to Mika. "Watch them," she commanded. Mika gave her a raised eyebrow but didn't argue. She ducked inside, warmth embracing her. It was nice to be out of the cold wind and near a hearth. There might not be one in the war tent, but she remembered seeing something of the sort in Asher's chambers.

Before she could give into her desire to find the roaring fire nearby, she whipped open the tent flap and stepped into the war tent.

Avalon stood from her seat the second their eyes met. Erik breathed a heavy sigh of relief and began making his way around the table. Before she could greet them, a sharp gasp met her ears.

"Is that—?" Sarin started to ask, but was cut off by Asher.

"Empress Danicka?"

Narra took a step inside to allow the empress to come out of hiding. Danicka lowered her hood, an impassive, bland look plastered on her face. Narra recognized the mask the empress wore. It was used to hide what she was really feeling —something Narra had far too much practice in.

"Good afternoon," Danicka said.

She barely got the words out before all hell broke loose.

10

Lasar shot forward faster than Narra had ever seen the man move before. Her heart pounded against her ribs as she tore her sword from its sheath just in time to block Lasar's straight sword. Cries of distress and confusion rang out around her, but she had no time to look around and see what was going on.

He growled close to her face, spittle flying from his lips. "I knew it! You're a *traitor*!"

Narra slammed her fist into his gut. Air exploded from his lungs as he doubled over. Before he could recover, she swept his legs out from under him and he crashed onto his back.

"Rheka!" Asher snapped. The rest of the voices had quieted, letting his voice ring clear through the tent.

Ignoring the general, Narra stepped onto Lasar's wrist, twisting her heel until the man winced. "Give up your blade, Lieutenant."

Lasar growled, and she ground her heel harder. With a yelp of pain, his fingers uncurled and Mika was able to snatch his sword from his hand. "Naizer *bitch*!"

Narra's fists curled as fire tore through her. "What did you just call me?" She kicked him hard in the side, and Lasar groaned as he rolled over, curling half way into the fetal position.

"Rheka, that's enough!" Asher grabbed her arm.

Narra glanced up in surprise. He'd been across the room a moment ago. She yanked her arm out of his grip and took a step back. Mika made a move to stand in front of her, but she raised a hand to stop him. "You expect me not to defend myself now?"

Asher sighed and rolled his eyes. "You had him subdued in seconds. You didn't need to kick him while was down too."

"You heard what he called me," she defended.

"I… did," Asher said slowly. "All the same."

Narra snorted. "His pride will heal."

Mika chuckled. "Unlikely."

Her lips started to quirk in a smile when Danicka cleared her throat. Narra glanced over her shoulder before looking back at the general.

"Grayson, meet Empress Danicka." Narra stepped to the side, allowing Danicka to face Asher. Narra kept her shoulders square with theirs, and her sword ready at her side. She had no idea how this was going to go down, or what Danicka would do.

If the empress made to attack Asher, she'd protect him, but if Asher tried to harm the empress, she felt compelled to defend the woman as well. Irritation warmed her belly. She didn't like this.

"Empress," Asher said. He nodded politely while scanning Danicka from head to toe. "I am General Asher Grayson, soon to be the next Emperor of Rova."

"Pleased to meet you," Danicka said. She scanned Asher with the same intensity. Neither of them offered their hand to shake. Instead, they stared each other down, quietly assessing the other like combatants before a fight.

"Rheka, please explain yourself," Asher said tightly.

Her stomach soured at his less-than-pleased tone. "Danicka and I had a rematch this morning. I won. We've struck a deal that gives Rova seven more days of reprieve from Kiznaiver attacks so we can fix our... internal problems."

Shocked murmurs passed through the room.

"That's... good news," Asher said, sounding impressed. He gave her a grateful look that warmed her belly and her cheeks at the same time.

"She's also offered to help us. In exchange, I have some information not pertinent to Rova that I'll be sharing with the empress," Narra added. "I think she could be an asset in the coming battle."

Danicka raised an eyebrow at Narra. "Coming battle, you say?"

Narra didn't bother answering. She didn't want to say more without Asher's permission. She stared meaningfully at Asher until he sighed and nodded. "She's agreed not to use any of the information she learns here against us."

Asher gave her a disbelieving look but turned to face the empress once more. "You swear to it, on your honor?"

Narra hid her smile. So Asher had picked up on Danicka's interesting quirk as well.

Danicka nodded. "I do."

"Sire, you can't believe a thing this woman says!" Gabriel spluttered. He was the first of Asher's subordinates to find his tongue.

Asher silenced the general with a look. "The former empress, Marina Kolarova, escaped custody and took over the Imperial Palace with the help of a small force of mercenaries," he explained to the empress. "With the time you've given us, we'll be able to lead a strong enough force back to the city and retake what's ours."

Danicka smiled. "What's ours, not *yours*?"

Asher's eyebrows furrowed in confusion.

Danicka shook her head before explaining. "You speak as if it won't all be yours one day soon. I like that. You view what happens to your people as something that happens to you personally, and vice versa."

Asher blinked in surprise. "Well, of course it is."

Danicka shrugged. "Not every emperor would agree."

"Only the good ones do," Narra said. She held Asher's intense stare until she could no longer stand the heat in his gaze.

"Agreed," Danicka said. "So I will help you retake your palace, and then we will return to the warfront."

Asher cleared his throat. "Yes."

"When do we leave?"

"Now," Asher said. "Can I trust you?"

"I won't do anything to harm you or yours unless provoked. Rheka and I have already come to this agreement.

Mason and I will obey it on our honor." Danicka shot her bodyguard a glance to ensure he nodded.

"Good, but you are aware I cannot simply trust your word," Asher added.

"I am," Danicka said.

"Rheka, can you watch them while they're with us?" Asher asked.

Narra nodded. She assumed she'd be in charge of Danicka and Mason. She had brought them into camp after all. "Of course."

"Thank you." Asher took a step back and regarded the rest of the room. "For now, we will put our faith in Empress Danicka. I won't hear any arguments on the matter." Several mouths slammed shut at this. "Now, we must prepare to leave. Gabriel, have three platoons withdrawn from our forces and prepared to depart. We'll take the horses and wagons to return to Rova City as quickly as possible."

"Yes, sire." Gabriel slipped out of the tent without another word.

"Sarin, take care of the horses and wagons. Have them prepared for departure in one hour," Asher said.

"Of course, sire." Sarin followed Gabriel from the tent.

"Lasar." Asher narrowed his eyes at the lieutenant still clutching his side. Lasar stood at the far side of the tent glaring at Narra. When Asher spoke his name, he finally forced his gaze away.

"Yes, sire?" Lasar asked.

"Your problem with Rheka ends today. You will not attack her again. That's an order."

Lasar's jaw hardened and he flashed a tight smile. "Of course, Your Majesty."

Asher held his stare for a few moments longer before he nodded. "Good. Everyone, pack your things and meet back here within the hour."

Narra nodded and watched as the rest of Asher and his men filed out of the tent, leaving Narra alone with Avalon, Erik, Mika, and their new Kiznai friends.

"You could tell me before you run off, you know." Avalon placed her hands on her hips.

Erik grinned. "She doesn't like worrying those she cares about."

Narra scoffed. "Of course I don't, and I knew you'd be safe here."

"I worried the moment I realized you were missing," Avalon shot back.

Narra closed her eyes. She wanted to groan. She didn't have time for this. Warm hands gripped hers, and she opened her eyes.

Avalon tightened her grip. "You might like to play the villain, but you really enjoy being the hero, don't you?"

Narra's cheeks heated. She'd never considered it. She didn't need to be known as anything but who she was, as long as she was known. "I only did what I had to."

"Because slipping into an enemy camp and challenging the empress of another country to a duel is 'what you had to do'?" Mika rolled his eyes.

Danicka laughed, surprising them all. Narra turned to look at the empress, who covered her mouth. She blushed prettily. "Apologies. I didn't mean to laugh. It just sounds like something I would do."

Mason grumbled something under his breath, not looking too pleased.

Narra couldn't help the small smile that spread on her face. "It seems we have more in common than I thought."

Danicka shrugged. "It seems we do."

"Let's go gather our things and get back here before the camp is in chaos," Avalon suggested. "We should beat the rush."

"Good idea." Narra waited for everyone to agree before she led the way out of the war tent and back across camp.

An hour later, Narra was squeezed between Asher and Avalon in the front seat of a steamwagon while Danicka, Mason, and Mika occupied the back seat.

At least she didn't have to sit on anyone's lap again. Stuck between two of the people she cared for most, Narra found it surprisingly easy to relax. She dozed off on Avalon's shoulder several times, only to be woken by the jostle of the steamwagon.

By morning she was feeling pretty well-rested, and ready to take on Marina's army.

Their soldiers assembled near the Barracks on the outskirts of town. Asher gave them time to rest while the war council met in the very room Narra had been captured in several months ago. She glanced around Asher's office and found the case for his jewel-encrusted rapier empty. It seemed like years ago she'd tried to steal it, only to be condemned and nearly hanged for a murder she hadn't committed.

As she inspected the stone walls and old portraits, she imagined it had been a whole other life when she'd been caught. It didn't feel like *her* that had been captured. That Narra was a totally different person. That Narra was angry and fuelled by grief. That Narra was even more reckless than the current one.

Narra wasn't that same person anymore, and she wasn't sure if she'd realized it until now.

"Marina's little army doesn't have the numbers," Gabriel said, forcing Narra to tune back into the conversation at hand. The general glanced at Danicka, who was inspecting a nearby bookshelf. The empress hardly seemed to be paying attention, yet every chance he got, Gabriel sent a suspicious glare her way.

"True," Sarin agreed, "but we still need to be careful."

"Of course," Asher said. "She must have scouts in the area, so I'm sure Marina knows we're coming."

"Then there's no point in preparing a sneak attack," Dom surmised.

"We're going to have to hit them head on," Therin guessed.

"Exactly," Asher said. "We'll hit them fast and hard. I'm sure Marina had the gates repaired, so we can blow the gates and force our way in. It'll be over in a matter of hours."

The Rovans exchanged triumphant glances.

"Are you sure it is wise to underestimate your opponent?" Danicka asked casually. She was still looking over the spines of books and didn't bother giving them her full attention.

"What do you mean?" Asher asked. "We were there when Marina took the palace. She barely had enough soldiers to defeat my Palace Guard."

"Mmm," Danicka hummed her agreement. "But who's to say she hasn't gathered more forces since you've been gone?"

Silence fell in the study. Asher exchanged wary glances with his council, considering Danicka's words.

"You may be right, Empress," Gabriel said. "But even if she could gather a few dozen more men, we have three military platoons. Whatever mercenaries she has been able to scrounge up can hardly hold a candle to my battle-tested men."

Danicka shrugged and made a dismissive noise with her nose. "It's as you say. I only mean you should proceed with caution."

"Anyway," Asher interjected as Gabriel's face turned bright red. "We'll proceed as planned with a full-scale attack on the Imperial Palace." He paused. "I can't believe I'm saying those words a second time."

Gabriel sighed, and the red tinting his cheeks faded. "I know the feeling, sire."

"We'll finish it this time. No more battles for the palace." Asher's jaw hardened. He braced his hands on his desk as he leaned over it, avoiding everyone's gaze.

Narra knew exactly what he meant. They would kill Marina Kolarova. There was no more leaving her alive. This time, she had to die.

The march of the army shook the cobblestone street as they made their way to the Imperial Palace at the top of the slope. Every shop they passed was closed, and fearful eyes peered between shutters. The people of Rova had no idea what was going on, but it'd all be over soon.

With over a hundred soldiers moving along the street and the two parallel to it, the rumble of the army shook the streets.

Her heart raced as the palace came into view. Stone spires shot up into the sky, while the steepled rooftops were just visible over the high outer wall. If they were on even ground, the castle might be easier to see, but with the slight curve of the road, it made the wall appear much taller than it was.

Soon they would be in battle. Narra went over the plan in her head one more time, even as adrenaline began pumping through her veins. Their orders were to push into the palace's courtyard as quickly as possible and hold the main battle there. No one wanted to see the livelihoods of the shop owners ruined because of this battle.

She looked at Asher, who marched alongside the rest of the army, a determined look on his face. Narra was sure Asher would try to help any shop owners affected by the battle, to recover; however, it might not be an expense the empire could afford. With the first coup, a battle for the palace, and an ongoing war, the military budget had to be stretched thin.

Her thoughts raced the closer they drew to the palace. Though she should be hiding in the alleys, moving quietly alongside her comrades, she couldn't bear to stick to the shadows and leave Asher to fend for himself. If she did, she'd be leaving Therin and Dom alone to protect their emperor. She couldn't do that. Though she trusted them to do their best, their best wasn't good enough to protect the emperor-to-be.

So even though it might get her killed, she walked a few paces behind Asher with her hood drawn over her head. Soldiers gave her curious looks as she walked among them, but they didn't spit or hiss at her pale skin or the strands of orange hair and fluttered around her face. It was almost like they'd grown to accept her.

Her gaze flicked up as a shadow leapt between shops in the corner of her eye. Erik watched from the rooftops, as per her suggestion. He'd be their eye in the sky should anything go wrong.

Avalon and Mika flanked her on either side while Danicka and Mason brought up the rear. While she hated having them directly behind her, she'd rather them than random soldiers, even if the soldiers didn't seem to mind her presence. Danicka could be trusted to keep her word: she wouldn't attack Narra given the chance. But the same couldn't be said for the Rovan soldiers.

She had to keep an eye on Danicka anyway. She was going to do her best to see to it that the empress got out of this alive. Hopefully, no Rovan soldiers would recognize the empress without her crown and signature whip. They'd even gone so far as to outfit the two Kiznai with Rovan clothes and weapons. At least they'd blend in.

As they reached the road that ringed the Imperial Palace's outer walls, the soldiers expanded along the line until they formed a loose circle, keeping the palace blocked in on all sides. The soldiers formed several rows, keeping a few yards back from the wall.

Narra stopped when Asher did, holding back a few rows away from the palace's outer doors, giving her a good view of the next stage of their plan.

A unit of soldiers filed out of the crowd with their shields up to protect them from anything that could be thrown down from above—be it arrows, boulders, or oil. They made their way slowly across the empty street to the large gates.

Narra scanned the top of the wall, but there were no guards in sight. Her eyebrows furrowed as she looked for their shadows, but there was *no one*. That was strange. If Marina was still occupying the palace, she should have guards on duty.

The active unit raised their shields higher and spread out to cover the two men rigging dynamite to the gates. Her eyes widened as she watched them work. It reminded her of the Boomers, though she wasn't sure she'd ever seen them use actual dynamite. August had far more creative concoctions he taught the thieves.

When the rigging was finished, the soldiers grouped up to protect the center two once more. One of the two soldiers slowly uncoiled a long wire as they returned to the rest of the army.

"On my command!" Asher shouted into the stillness that lay over Rova City. No one spoke. No one moved as they awaited Asher's order. "Ready defenses!" As one, the army shifted. The front ranks dropped to one knee and positioned their shields in front of them while the rows behind them raised their shields over their heads. Such a maneuver would block any shrapnel from pelting their ranks. "On my count!"

Again, the street fell into silence. It was as if everyone collectively holding their breath as they waited. The only sound Narra could make out was the pounding of her heart in her ears.

"Three! Two! One! Now!"

Narra ducked instinctively as the roar of an explosion shook the surrounding street. Buildings trembled and stone cracked against stone. Pieces of wood and iron pelted the shields around her as well as the shops on either side of the street.

Her breaths quickened as she waited and listened. Ringing built in her ears from the massive noise. Her eyebrows furrowed and she shook her head. The ringing slowly subsided, and she straightened to peer over the shields still lying flat overtop the rows of soldiers.

The palace gates were blown apart with only the hinges left swaying precariously from either side of the dark stone walls. Smoke wafted across the street and small bits of flame ate at some of the wood closest to the open gateway.

As the smoke began to recede, the courtyard inside of the walls was slowly revealed. The points of spears became visible first, and then the metal helmets of soldiers with a black feather sticking from them instead of the red of Rova's soldiers came into view.

When the smoke cleared completely, Narra was left staring at a small army inside the palace walls—and none of them were moving.

A shiver descended her spine and cold wrapped around her lungs. She didn't like this. Something was wrong. The mercenaries were still, like frozen sculptures. Their eyes stared unseeing at the sea of shields before them. A few had flaming bits of wood on their shoulders, orange sparks catching on their dry hair. Even as one man's face began to blacken with burns, no one moved.

"What's wrong with them?" Avalon murmured, her fear echoing Narra's.

Asher looked around at his men and then back through the open gates. His fists curled at his sides. He didn't like this either, but what could they do? They couldn't retreat. They still had the numbers. Plus, now that the gate was down, all they had to do was take the palace and subdue or kill Marina's mercenaries.

When Asher didn't make a move after another long moment, Narra leaned forward and gently laid her hand on his back. He jumped and sent her a questioning look over his shoulder.

"You need to give an order," she whispered, hoping only he could hear her. She didn't want Asher's soldiers to think she was calling the shots, but he needed to do something.

Asher gave her a barely perceptible nod, then faced forward again. "First Platoon!" His shout rang clear down the street. "Charge!"

In unison, the rows of soldiers around Narra maneuvered their shields from overhead, positioning them in front of themselves. A battle cry rose up, and then everyone around her pushed forward. As planned, Narra was swept up with the First Platoon. If Asher insisted on going into battle, then so did she and her friends. Avalon wouldn't stay behind this time, so Narra had told Mika to protect the pirate too. If Avalon emerged unscathed, she'd told him she would try and reach out to her mother. It was unlikely that Narra would go through with it, but Mika didn't know that.

Bodies pushed all around her, jostling her into both Mika and Avalon as they pressed forward. The line of soldiers narrowed to fit through the gates and then spread out again. The clang of swords rang through the courtyard as the fighting began.

As the First Platoon spread out into the space, mercenaries surged through the cracks. Narra shot Mika a look of warning, telling him silently to watch Avalon. She received a tiny nod before she slipped up to join Asher, Therin, and Dom.

"Watch him," Narra commanded them.

Therin and Dom didn't even blink at her demanding

attitude anymore. They dipped their chins in understanding, while Asher sighed heavily. He could be upset with her protectiveness all he wanted, as long as he survived. Without him, this country would fall into chaos. He was the key to peace. There was no way she could let him die today.

A mercenary cut through the soldier in front of her, sending blood spilling across the once pristine cobblestone.

Narra pushed forward before he could get his bearings. She sliced through his throat as more enemies surged forward, then danced away as a second lunged. Her heart raced as she dodged two slashes before meeting his sword high in the air. While his arms were up, she yanked a dagger from her belt and drove it between his chest and hip plates. Red blood gushed hot against her hand, and she quickly yanked her weapon free.

She got a quick glimpse of the dead look in his eyes before he collapsed. Then she was on to the next enemy.

Soldiers fought opponents on all sides. Even Therin and Dom had to step forward and block an opponent each. A third snuck around the side of them, but Asher saw him coming and quickly killed him.

Only when the mercenary was dead on the ground did she breath easier.

"Narra!" Avalon's sharp voice warned.

She spun, her sword flying up to meet the blade of her next opponent. She inhaled sharply and ground her teeth as the burly woman pushed down on her blade. Though Narra was strong, she couldn't compete with the sheer size of the female mercenary. She had to be over six feet tall with thighs like tree trunks and arms like the thickest branches she'd ever seen.

Narra leapt back to get space between them, but the mercenary woman shot forward. She threw a punch at Narra's gut, but the thief twisted away, sliding their blades down each other with a sharp *shing*. The sound rang in her ears as she artfully spun to avoid another swipe of the mercenary woman's sword.

Thunder cracked overhead, and Narra's heart leapt with fear. That had to be Avalon. What was going on? She wanted desperately to turn and find out but doing so might cost Narra her life. She ground her teeth, anger flaring hot through her chest. She swiped the woman's sword sideways, parrying her. Narra lunged, but before she could end it, a sword was thrust through the mercenary's stomach from behind.

She blinked in surprise as the large woman dropped, and Avalon appeared on her other side, sword extended and covered in blood.

"You saved me," Narra said, stunned.

The fury in Avalon's eyes faded as soon as their eyes met. She grinned from ear to ear and winked at the thief. "You're welcome."

Narra didn't get the chance to say thank you. Therin was pushed between them, almost stumbling onto his backside. A mercenary trudged forward, only to have his knee taken out by Avalon's swift kick. The man toppled to his good knee with a cry of pain. Narra cut off his cry with a slam of her dagger through one of his eye sockets. He dropped hard, bouncing a little on the cobblestone.

"Thanks," Therin said through harsh breaths. "That was a strong one."

"No problem," Narra and Avalon said in unison.

Therin gave them both a strange look before his eyes widened. Narra spun in time to see a crack in their forward team. Mercenaries were spilling through the soldiers on the frontline, heading straight for Asher.

Narra's heart pounded hard as she dove to protect him. Therin and Avalon were quick on her heels. Narra braced herself and threw her shoulder hard into the first soldier, sending him flying into a pair with locked swords. The three of them yelped as they tumbled to the ground, while Narra spun to face whoever dared raise their sword next.

Her blade slammed against her next opponent's, but he was far weaker than he appeared and fell quickly under her rapid strikes. She decapitated the next mercenary before throwing several knives in quick succession.

"Keep going, men!" Asher shouted. He received a round of battle cries in response. The Rovans were winning, just as they had expected.

Narra flashed an adrenaline fuelled grin and went back at it. She cut through every opponent she could, helping the army push farther and farther into the courtyard until they were nearly at the palace steps. Her heart pounded hard and sweat poured down her back. She was having the time of her life.

With each strike, they grew closer to victory. For every mercenary the soldiers downed, it was one less man that stood against Narra and blocked her from exacting her final revenge against the former Empress of Rova.

Narra sliced a mercenary's neck, sending a spray of blood over her and the surrounding soldiers. The man clutched at his throat, his eyes going wide. Narra smiled as she slammed her boot into his abdomen, sending him flying back onto the first step up to the castle's front doors.

She howled in victory as she charged forward. She nearly made it to the first step when the front doors cracked open.

Narra froze, squeezing her sword in one hand and dagger in the other. Her eyebrows furrowed as the palace doors opened wide and Marina stepped out.

She's surrendering! Narra's eyes widened and excitement flooded her body. She began to move up to the next stair when Marina stepped aside to allow another woman to emerge from behind her.

Narra fell back a step, shock slamming into her like a train. She couldn't breathe. She couldn't move. Cold flooded her body and froze her limbs. This couldn't be happening. Not in a thousand years did she imagine this fate.

Ashra smirked down at Narra from the top of the tall staircase. Her dark blue eyes flashed with malicious delight.

"Rheka!" Someone called for her, but Narra couldn't figure out who it was. Her brain was working too slowly. She tried to push forward, to catch up to what was happening, but she couldn't move through the fog suddenly slowing her.

"Narra!" someone else yelled.

Swords clashed around her. People were protecting her from the attacking mercenaries. No matter how much she knew she needed to keep fighting, she couldn't. She couldn't even blink or look away from the Goddess of Death staring her dead in the eye.

"*Daughter*," Ashra purred, throwing more ice over the cold already clutching Narra tight in its grasp.

"Death bringer, get a hold of yourself!"

Narra blinked through the fog, but she still couldn't look away from those awful eyes. The eyes that told her this was over. She'd lost. She'd bet against the wrong team. She'd been fighting for the wrong monarch. Because no matter what was right in the world—no matter what was best for Rova—no one could stand up to Lady Death.

"Narra, please!" Avalon grabbed Narra's arm and tried yanking her back.

Ashra cackled, her voice drowning out the almost deafening sounds of battle. Narra winced as pain shot through her ears. She moved to clamp her hands over them, but then the sound stopped.

The Goddess of Death lifted a hand, her fingers moving through the air like she was casting a spell. The black of her dress started to spill down the steps like ink, drowning all the gray stone around it until it parted around Narra. It slipped across the cobblestone courtyard and up the legs of Rovan soldiers.

Narra looked around in horror, finally free from the spell of Ashra's gaze. Black tendrils worked their way up the Rovan soldiers' bodies until the soldiers spasmed and then froze like statues. Their eyes were completely black.

The battle around her died almost immediately, except for her friends' fights. Asher continued to war with a mercenary, as did Mika and Avalon. Even Erik had joined them at some point, but none of them seemed affected.

Then she realized Therin and Dom had stopped moving. Their gazes were black and unseeing.

Her heart pounded hard as the cold finally gave way to some semblance of feeling. Narra looked back up at Ashra, then Marina. The former empress smiled as their gazes met, and then she looked out over the courtyard.

Spreading her arms wide, Marina laughed softly. "Fight for me!"

The Rovan soldiers stiffened and then slowly jerked into motion. Their movements were similar to the mercenaries', but far slower. They closed in on her friends and the soldiers still fighting in the back. Not all of their allies had been put under control, only the dozens upon dozens closest to the steps. Did Ashra's mind control have a proximity limit?

"Retreat," Narra whispered. Her breathing grew labored as she spun, catching the attention of her friends. "We need to retreat!"

Asher gave her a confused look before his gaze slipped over the top of her head. He saw the black oozing from Ashra's dress, and then he looked at the black in his soldiers' eyes.

Narra didn't need to prompt him further. Asher backpedalled, pushing through a few of their former allies without trouble. It seemed he understood quickly enough.

"Retreat!" Asher bellowed. Again, he stepped back, but this time, a mercenary caught his arm.

Narra yanked a throwing knife from her belt and tossed it before she even registered what she was doing. The knife slammed into the mercenary's skull, and he dropped lifeless to the cobblestone.

Asher gave her a grateful look before he turned to begin the retreat back to the gates. Only now dozens of zombie-like soldiers surrounded them. They were mindless, jerking forward, but not attacking—yet. How long did they have until they *did* attack?

It could be seconds, or minutes. Either way, they needed to go *now*.

"Let's go!" Narra yelled. She grabbed Avalon and pushed her forward after Asher. Mika was quick to follow, and then Erik brought up the rear.

Narra was only a few steps behind when someone grabbed her elbow and yanked her back. She spun and slashed her sword out, right through Therin's throat.

She gasped and went still as drops of blood splattered her cheeks. Therin didn't even grab his throat—he just fell. She knelt down next to him. She reached out to grab his throat and hold back the flow of blood. She wanted to help him, to keep him from dying. He was one of *them*. But then Dom grabbed her shoulder. His eyes were entirely black when she looked at him. Her pulse pounded as he raised his sword.

"Dom," she whispered. The man didn't hesitate in bringing his blade down towards her.

Narra rolled back, pulling from his grip before leaping up onto her feet. Dom blinked like he wondered where she'd gone, then slowly followed her progression. He took a slow step forward, then two.

"Dom, stop!" Narra yelled. "Snap out of it!"

Dom took another step, lumbering closer until he could swipe at her again. She easily jumped out of the way, but then multiple Rovan soldiers were reaching for her, each with black eyes and a slack look on their face.

"Narra!" Erik called. She heard him pushing through enemies as he raced to rescue her.

She'd just killed Therin, one of their allies, and she couldn't save Dom. She couldn't save any of them. The soldiers had disappeared into Ashra's spell.

"I'm coming," Narra whispered. Her mind raced and her pulse pounded. She spun on her heel and pushed through the slowly animating soldiers around her. She slammed into Erik, pushing her best friend right back the way he'd come. "Go!" she screamed.

Erik took off, flying on the heels of Danicka and Mason, who she hadn't realized were still with them. *Ancestors*. She'd been so busy protecting Asher and pushing the battle forward that she hadn't even looked to see if Danicka was faring okay.

But she didn't have time to chastise herself now. Now, she had to run.

Erik continued to push their way through the crowd until the clash of swords met her ears again. She hadn't realized it had died out, but now that she did, it started back up again with a vengeance.

Suddenly, Rovan soldiers at the back of the courtyard warred with the zombies from the front. Confused looks passed over their faces as they pushed back their brethren.

"What are you doing?" one shouted.

"Stop! We're not the enemy!" another soldier yelled.

Every desperate cry was met with silence. Their allies turned on them and attacked. The zombies were slow and lacked precision with every blow, but they gave a few unprepared Rovans some nasty gashes.

Several cries of pain rose from the men around them.

"Retreat!" Asher shouted from somewhere up ahead.

Soldiers began to surge backward, pushing Narra left and right. A sword nicked her side, and rough hands grabbed her arm, but she pushed and pulled until she was free every time.

"We've got to get out of here!" Narra yelled at Erik's back.

He nodded as he reached back to grab her hand. She slipped her hand into his, only to have a large body slam into her side.

She flew sideways, taking out two other soldiers beside her. The soldiers cushioned her fall, but whoever ran into her had succeeded in knocking the air from her lungs. She gasped for breath and struggled to stand.

A body landed on top of her, and strong hands gripped her throat.

Panic shot through her. She reached for her sword, but it had been lost somewhere in her fall. She couldn't find it, and as the pain began to grow, she realized she needed to breathe. She needed *air*. She clawed at the man's fingers, but they didn't budge. Just as Narra began to feel lightheaded, he went limp.

She gasped for air as his hands loosened. Then the body rolled off her and a pale hand reached for her.

"Are you all right?" Danicka asked. Her brows knitted together with worry, but her eyes darted everywhere around them. She wasn't letting her guard down for a second.

"Yeah," Narra choked. She coughed as she took Danicka's hand and let the empress yank her to her feet.

"Come on!" Danicka tugged Narra through the crowd. They ducked and dodged as Rovans faced off against each other. It was complete anarchy as they tried to push through to the back of the crowd and break onto the street without being cut or stabbed.

Just as she spotted a head of curly brown hair bouncing at the edge of the fight, a swarm of bodies pushed up against her on all sides, and she lost her grip on Danicka's hand. The crowd surged, and battle cries rang out. She gritted her teeth as she turned to face her next opponent.

Narra swung around, cutting through the next zombie-like soldier to grip her arm. Her chest heaved as she took a moment's reprieve. She looked around, spotting her friends farther away. They were amongst the soldiers not possessed by Ashra, so at least they were safe for now.

A feminine cry broke through her thoughts, and she spun to find Danicka grappling with another enemy while two more rushed from either side. The empress managed to slip from the grip of the first soldier before slicing her dagger across his throat and kicking him in the gut. Her momentum sent her reeling back into the arms of another enemy. He moved to grab her throat, but Danicka spun away. The third soldier caught her wrist, and panic widened her eyes.

Narra's heart raced as she pushed through enemy and friendly soldiers alike. She gritted her teeth as she cut through zombie-soldiers and then slammed into the mercenary who had grabbed Danicka's wrist.

She fell to the ground on top of the soldier and swiftly stabbed him twice in the back of the neck before she leapt to her feet.

Danicka twisted in the grip of another soldier grabbing her arms, but from the empress' wince, his grip was iron-like.

Narra grabbed Danicka's shoulder and jolted her back towards a friendly, non-zombie soldier. The empress yelped as a mercenary reached for her, grabbing a silver locket around her neck.

The chain tore and the necklace fell to the bloody ground.

Narra surged after the empress and pushed her in the direction of Mason whose head had appeared at the edge of the crowd. Damn that man was tall.

Danicka twisted in Narra's grip to look over her shoulder. "My locket!" Her wide blue eyes shone with terror. She dug in her heels, stopping a few feet from her bodyguard.

"What are you doing?" Narra growled. "We need to get out of here."

"Not without my locket!" Danicka said. Her chest heaved with her quick breaths. Though Danicka didn't look strained physically, she was breathing like she'd just run a marathon.

"You can replace a damn necklace," Narra snapped. She pushed Danicka towards Mason, but the empress dug in her heels again.

"You don't understand!" Danicka's breathing continued to quicken until she was holding a hand to her chest like she couldn't breathe.

Narra's eyebrows furrowed. She'd seen someone have a panic attack before, but she had no idea how to stop it. "Calm down!" Narra grabbed Danicka's arms and forced the empress to look her in the eye. "It's just a necklace."

Danicka shook her head. "It's not just a necklace! It's the only picture I have of my mother! I won't leave without it."

Narra blinked in surprise. She couldn't imagine wanting choosing a trinket over her own safety.

"Your Majesty!" Mason appeared at Danicka's shoulder.

The empress reached back to grip his arm for support. Narra hadn't realized it before, but Danicka was shaking like a leaf.

"I'll get your damn necklace," Narra spat. Better her than the empress. If Danicka died, it'd mean all out war with Kiznaiver. At least with the empress alive, they might be able to find a peaceful resolution when this was all over.

Danicka's eyes widened. "You will?"

Narra nodded. She gently pushed Danicka back into Mason's arms. "Take her out of here and meet up with the others." She met Mason's green eyes, giving him a stern look until he agreed with a nod.

"Good luck," Mason said.

Narra snorted and turned back to the battlefield. She heard faint mutters as the two Kiznai slipped off into the crowd of soldiers, but she didn't pay them any mind. She couldn't believe she was about to go back in there for a damn necklace. But she wasn't about to break a promise.

Yanking a dagger from her belt, Narra pushed back through the crowd. She'd last seen the locket only a few meters away. If she could get in and out quickly, she'd be able to catch up with the others. She was sure by now that Erik, Avalon, and Mika would be looking for her. She wouldn't risk their lives for a damn trinket.

A mercenary jumped in her path, and Narra cut through him without hesitation. It was easier to kill the mercenaries. They were traitors to the crown, but the Rovan soldiers were more difficult to kill. She was sure they didn't want this. They were being used and abused by Marina and Ashra.

An angry growl rumbled in her chest as she ducked a punch from a zombie-soldier. Weaving through the crowd, she stayed low and killed where she had to until she returned to the spot she'd last seen the locket.

Her gaze raked the ground at her feet while she simultaneously fought off her assailants. Blood sprayed her clothes and the ground, hot drops of red hitting her cheeks as she stabbed the throat of a zombie-soldier.

A flash of silver caught her eye. It was about damn time.

In one smooth motion, Narra ducked and rolled, snatching the locket from the ground as she did. She opened her palm slightly as she dove back between friendly soldiers.

The metal clasp was broken. She hardly made it a few steps before she thumbed open the locket and froze mid step.

Her pounding heart stopped as blue eyes met hers. It was just a photo, but she'd know that face anywhere. Her father stood next to a woman much like Danicka. They stood slightly apart but still held hands while giving the camera an awkward smile.

What was this? And why did Danicka have it?

Her heart started back up too fast, making her chest ache.

She took a few tentative steps forward, her mind racing with possibilities.

Cold wrapped around her. She knew she was in shock, but she had to keep going. She had to get out of there and get to the others.

Slowly, she made her way through the warring soldiers. The Rovans were falling back, but many still fought so their brothers and sisters could escape.

When she finally pushed free of the soldiers, her body was numb, and her mind was stuttering to catch up. She pictured the photo in her mind over and over. She didn't need to look at it to see the image again. It was burned into her mind like a brand.

"Narra!" Avalon slammed into her, grabbing her biceps and squeezing hard. "Are you all right?" Her brown eyes raked Narra from head to toe.

Narra nodded mutely and pulled from Avalon's grip. She didn't say a word as she headed towards Asher, Erik, Mika, and the two Kiznai that were part of their team.

"We need to find a safe place to hide," Asher was saying to Erik.

Erik dipped his chin. His eyes were hard as he stared at Asher. "We should return to Narra's apartment."

She sighed. Her best friend still hated the general, but at least he wasn't trying to kill him again.

Asher grunted his agreement and turned to face Narra as she joined them.

She didn't say a word, only passed by them on the way to the alley behind them. Footsteps followed the thief as she led them farther and farther away from battle. They still had to get to safety before she could think about what the image in the locket meant, but with every step she took, more questions burned to the surface of her mind.

If that photo meant what she thought it did, then Narra had a sister. She shook her head to push away the thought. She had no blood relation left but Alden. Khlara wasn't part of her life anymore—she was dead to Narra. Only the family she'd created between her, Erik, and Alden was left. And that's all she needed.

"What about your soldiers?" Danicka asked someone behind her.

Asher sighed. "I sounded the retreat to the Barracks. They'll be safe there until we come up with a new plan."

"We?" Danicka sounded amused.

"The rest of us," Asher corrected.

The sound of Danicka's voice had heat flaring through Narra's chest. Rage ate up the cold and tightened her fists. How dare this woman even speak? What else was she hiding? What other secrets did she have that threatened to tear Narra to pieces? Because that's what this felt like. She couldn't think, couldn't speak, and couldn't breathe through the heat coiling around her lungs.

"Surely you wouldn't deny my help," Danicka teased.

Narra swung around. Before she could regain her usual logic, she grabbed Danicka by the shoulders and slammed her up against the wall. Danicka gasped and winced from the pain of the impact. Narra held her forearm over Danicka's windpipe, pressing firmly while she slapped her palm against the wall next to Danicka's head. The locket dangled from where it wrapped around her thumb, silver flashing even in the low light.

"Why in Srah's name do you have a picture of my father?" Narra growled. Her chest heaved and her hands trembled until she fisted them. She felt like she was about to crack, like the whole world might shatter around her.

Confusion furrowed Danicka's brows. Narra heard the draw of swords behind her and a small scuffle as someone must have grabbed Mason to hold him back. Danicka glanced over Narra's shoulder before her eyes were drawn back to the locket, and the half folded photo stuffed into the frame.

The empress' eyes widened in surprise as she made the connection. Their gazes met. They had the same blue eyes—the eyes they both shared with Quinn Reiner.

"Who are you?" Danicka breathed out the words, her voice hitching.

Narra stepped back abruptly, a snarl leaving her lips. She began to pace up and down the alley. Everyone stuck to the edges, their eyes wide and faces filled with confusion.

"How is this even possible?" Narra yelled, throwing up her hands. She spun to face Danicka, who was being checked on by Mason.

Danicka pushed away her bodyguard and met Narra's gaze. They both winced at the same time. How had they not seen it before? It was like looking into a mirror.

"I never knew my father," Danicka said slowly and softly, like she was trying to calm a startled beast. "My mother always said it was better that way—that it was just a fling. My father... Quinn. He confessed to my mother after they'd... had relations, that he couldn't take care of his own daughter. So, when he left and my mother discovered she was pregnant, she decided not to contact him. She thought I'd be better off not knowing him. She never saw or heard from him again."

Narra's heart pounded hard. She didn't remember a time when her father had left for a long time. Had he gone to Kiznaiver, or had Danicka's mother come to Rova City? When had they met? They were three years apart in age. So her father had an affair when she was still a child?

It was ridiculous, and it also made total sense. Her father was a destructive man. How many other families did he ruin? How many other women had he gotten pregnant? For all she knew, she could have dozens of brothers and sisters.

The heat of her rage cooled, and a different kind of warmth bubbled to the surface. A laugh burst from her chest. It was manic and disturbed even her.

"I can't fucking believe this," Narra said. Another laugh bubbled from her throat. "That bastard. That *fucking bastard.*"

Erik approached her slowly. She didn't flinch when he took her arm and squeezed gently. He pulled her gaze to his. His eyes were dark and his forehead was wrinkled. He was more worried than she'd ever seen him.

"I'm fine," Narra said quickly. "I'm fucking fine."

Erik didn't protest when she pulled away. She almost took up pacing again, but before she could turn on her heel and start back down the alley, a shadow appeared at the end, making her freeze.

Ria rushed down the alley, kicking up pebbles as she went. She breathed hard, her eyes wild as she collided with Narra. She grabbed Narra's arms and sighed in relief. "Thank Ashra I found you."

"Ria?" Narra blinked in surprise as she held the elbows of the assassin, keeping her steady as she caught her breath. Ria sounded like she'd been running a marathon from the way she was breathing. It had to be serious if Ria was in such distress. "What's going on?"

Ria gulped down air, taking a full minute to get herself together. "Not here."

Narra's eyebrows furrowed. She didn't have time for this. Though Ria's presence had thrown cold water on her rising hysteria, she could still feel it at the edge of her mind, waiting to take hold. "Just tell me."

Ria shook her head. "It's not safe."

Narra sighed. "Fine. Come with us." They were on their way to her apartment anyway. Maybe once they arrived, Ria would divulge whatever it was she was keeping a secret.

Ria glanced over Narra's shoulder and her eyes widened

slightly in surprise like she hadn't noticed all the people flanking her. "You're coming from the palace?" she guessed.

Narra nodded.

"All right, let's be quick." Ria turned on her heel and walked briskly to the end of the alley.

Narra shot a confused look over her shoulder before following the assassin.

Ten minutes later, Narra closed the vault-like door to her apartment behind her. She didn't bother locking it yet, as she wasn't sure they were all staying. She walked into the living room where Ria perched on the edge of the couch, rubbing her hands nervously up and down her thighs.

"Out with it," Narra said. She folded her arms over her chest. She wanted to thank Ria for interrupting when she did. She couldn't mentally handle the revelation of having a sister yet. She'd much rather focus on a different problem.

Ria glanced around at the rest of the group. Mika leaned against the wall closest to the door while Avalon and Erik hovered by the kitchen doorway like they wanted to say something. Asher waited in the living room, his hand on the hilt of his sword, and the Kiznai stood farthest down the hall, exchanging confused looks with one another.

When Ria finally met Narra's gaze again, fear flashed through the assassin's eyes. Cold wrapped around Narra and she shivered. She'd never seen Ria afraid before. What could be so bad that even a servant of the Goddess of Death would tremble?

"There's something I need to tell you about Ashra," Ria said tentatively.

The Kiznai stirred, confusion marring their faces.

"Was that her, at the palace?" Erik asked. Narra nodded mutely. "That's why you froze."

Avalon inhaled sharply. "That was her? The Goddess of Death?"

"She was the one controlling my men?" Asher growled, looking angry and terrified all at once.

"What are you talking about?" Danicka snapped. She stepped away from Mason, her hands curling into fists. "I won't allow you to desecrate the name of Lady Death. She is a god. She is to be respected and revered, just like Srah."

Narra exchanged a look with Ria before looking back at Danicka. "That was her, Danicka."

Danicka froze. Her jaw set stubbornly at the same time fear widened her eyes. "You're lying."

"No, she isn't," Ria said. "I'm Ria, one of the Daughters of Ashra." She nodded at Narra. "Narra is one of us too."

"I don't believe you."

Narra sighed. "I don't care." She looked at Ria. "Tell me what's going on."

Ria turned away from the empress and began rubbing her sweaty palms on her thighs once more. "Ashra is leaking chaos."

Narra raised an eyebrow. That didn't sound good. "What does that mean?"

"It's happened throughout history, but I've only seen it once before." Ria's eyes darkened and she cast her gaze on the floor. "It was only a few years after my sisters and I pledged ourselves to the goddess."

Narra waited for Ria to continue, her heart pounding.

"The last time this happened, Ashra had to choose another host to inhabit. She picked Mona."

Narra gasped involuntarily. "Your sister?"

Ria nodded gravely. "Mona became a zealot for Ashra long before she was chosen. She did whatever, whenever Ashra asked. She's the reason our little sister is dead. Ashra isn't my Mona anymore, but I know she's still in there."

"What are you saying?"

"When Mona ascended to god status, her mind joined with all the Ashra's before her. My Mona is still in there, but with Ashra bleeding chaos energy, she's losing her power, and that's making her act destructively," Ria explained.

Narra clenched her fists, digging her nails into her palms to stave off the sudden dizziness threatening to send her to the ground.

"If Ashra doesn't get a new body fast, she might be too weak to switch," Ria continued.

Narra looked up sharply. "You want me to help you find her a new host?"

Ria winced. Guilt flashed through her eyes. "No. Ashra has already chosen Marina."

Fire flared through her, consuming her every thought. "After all that witch has done to me, Ashra has decided to make my enemy her next host?" Betrayal burned a path through Narra until she saw red. This couldn't be happening. Why did every person in her life seek to betray her?

Ria grunted some kind of agreement. "Yes. But she originally chose you, Narra." Her gaze flickered between the people standing around them. It was clear Ria didn't want to say all of this in front of them, but Narra was giving her no choice. She needed to know *everything*. Now.

"When did she choose me?" Narra growled.

"You remember your ceremony?" Ria asked. "That's why it was so... intense. Ashra chose you the moment she met you. She feeds on chaos and she thought you would be the best to continue her legacy—until she found Marina. It isn't natural for a human to act so... chaotic. Ashra was drawn to her, and as you grew more and more entrenched in Marina's plots, Mother decided she wanted to be the next Empress of Rova."

"This is madness!" Danicka snapped. "You can't believe these lies!"

The empress met Narra's eyes, but Narra only shook her head. Danicka didn't understand. "When you meet Lady Death for yourself, maybe you'll understand."

Danicka took a step back like Narra had slapped her.

"What can we do?" Erik asked. His voice was higher than usual. He was afraid. "How can we win against a god?"

Narra looked back at Ria. "Any ideas?"

Ria's eyebrows rose. There were tears behind her eyes. The thief took a step forward, laying her hand gently on Ria's elbow. "We need to kill Ashra."

Narra's heart raced even as it was clear Ria's broke. "How?"

Ria shook her head. "I don't know. We could let her time run out—keep Marina away from her."

Narra nodded. She looked over her shoulder and met Asher's frightened gaze. "We take the palace, and we kill Marina."

Asher's mouth pressed into a firm line. Resignation settled in his eyes. He didn't argue. He didn't say a thing.

"How?" Avalon spoke up. "We already tried that and the army was taken."

"Easy." Narra smiled ruefully. "We sneak in like thieves."

NARRA SAT beside Danicka on the couch later that night. Asher had disappeared not long after Ria had left, heading off to do gods only knew what. They had come up with a tentative plan: create a distraction and sneak into the palace. There was more to it than that, but Narra's mind was sluggish in her tired haze. There was so much to think about that she could hardly focus on the coming days.

Tomorrow they would prepare. The next day they would act.

Narra sighed. She stared into the hearth, soft snores surrounding her. Neither woman could sleep. Narra had tried, but after tossing and turning for hours, she had gotten up to get tea, only to find Danicka sitting on the couch, staring into the hearth with unseeing eyes.

The thief had sat down beside the empress, and neither of them had spoken once. Twenty minutes later, they still stared straight ahead. It wasn't comfortable silence. There was too much tension in the air. But Narra didn't know what to say. They were sisters. Blood. They were family, even if they only shared one parent. How had this happened?

"So Lady Death is real," Danicka finally said. Her voice was soft, almost a whisper.

It seemed their thoughts were in very different places. Narra glanced at the empress. "Yes, she is."

Danicka kneaded the edge of her shirt and sighed. "I always knew she was real, but I never thought I'd see her in the flesh."

"You knew gods were real?" Narra's forehead wrinkled in confusion.

"Of course," Danicka said. "But I wasn't just taught to believe in the gods, like you might have been as a child. Like you, I've met a god before."

Narra looked at her with wide eyes. "Have you met Srah, then?"

Danicka's eyes widened to mirror Narra's own. "No. Have you?" Narra nodded and Danicka's mouth dropped open. "You're a very lucky woman."

Narra snorted. "I wouldn't say that."

"You are," Danicka said stubbornly. "But there aren't only two gods. From what I understand, all gods were once flesh, and when they die they become gods in the spirit realm. Their bones still litter our lands."

Realization hit Narra. "Your crown."

Danicka's lips curved. "Yes. My crown was made from the bones of a Spirit God of Nature. Your dagger was made from the same kind of bones, though whose, I couldn't say."

Narra wanted to go to her room and grab the dagger. She wanted to sit and inspect it for hours while she tried to figure out its secrets. Did Ashra kill another god to create it? It made sense. But why would she do that? Were gods at war? How many gods were there? A million questions flew through her mind.

"You really had no idea, did you?" Danicka tilted her head, making her white hair spill over her shoulder.

"No," Narra said. "Ashra gave it to me to kill my mother."

Again, Danicka's eyes widened. "She wants you to kill your mother?"

Narra nodded. "She wants to be the only *mothe*r in my life." Resentment dripped from her voice, burning like acid up her throat. She wanted to retch. She hated the idea of killing her own mother, even if Khlara had betrayed her. Ashra's possessiveness was disturbing.

"Ah, she calls herself your Mother. That's what your assassin friend meant. She calls you her Daughters, correct?"

"Yes."

"What a strange thing to do," Danicka said.

Narra smiled. "I couldn't agree more." She paused, sliding her gaze from the hearth over to the empress. "So do you know what Ria means about this chaos business?"

Danicka frowned and shook her head. "No. I have no idea."

Narra nodded and leaned back against the couch. She stared into the flickering flames, her racing heart slowly settling.

"So, we're sisters," Danicka said.

Narra's heart leapt. "So we are."

"I always wanted a sister," Danicka said softly.

Narra wasn't sure if she was meant to hear that.

"You'll wish you hadn't when you get to know me," Narra joked.

Danicka laughed. Her voice was sweet and soft. She muffled her laugh with her hand. They both froze, giving a quick look around the room. Erik continued to snore softly. He lay on a thick blanket behind the couch, while Mika was propped up against the wall nearby. From the flare of his nostrils, Narra was sure he wasn't asleep any longer, but she didn't say anything.

Exhaustion lay on her mind like a fog, threatening to pull her under. It was time she returned to bed with Avalon.

Narra sighed and stood up. "We can discuss this tomorrow... whatever this is."

Danicka nodded slightly, but she didn't stand to see Narra off. She only watched as the thief stepped around the couch, avoiding Erik's feet peeking from beneath his blanket. "Good night, Narra."

Narra stilled. She hadn't told Danicka she could call her that, but then again, the empress was her sister. Instead of berating her, Narra smiled. "Good night, Danicka."

"For the last time, you cannot come into the Guild with us," Narra said. She narrowed her eyes at Mika, who continued to grin mischievously.

"But I'd love to see how your Thieves Guild works," Mika said. "And what if I want to join?"

Narra scoffed at the same time Erik snort-laughed. "You're an assassin!"

"And? So are you." Mika flashed his teeth.

Narra stared at the ceiling and clenched her fists. She slowly counted down from ten, trying to keep her anger leashed. She wanted nothing more than to hit this stupid man.

"*Do* you want to join?" Narra challenged.

"Maybe."

"Then as the Guild Master, I deny your potential request to join our ranks." Narra marched ahead with Erik, leaving Mika to stare after them with the smile wiped from his face.

After a moment of stunned silence, Mika caught back up with them. They walked the cold tunnel between Rova City and the manor. They were nearly there, and she still hadn't convinced Mika to wait in the sewer.

"Guild Master?" Mika questioned. "I thought you said you were a commander."

"She's both." Erik chuckled.

"So I should really be calling you Master Rheka, or is it *Mistress*?" Mika's grin returned, making Narra groan.

"You'll call me nothing. You'll say nothing. You'll hide in this damn sewer while I meet with the commanders." Narra glared into the darkness ahead. She'd grown tired of looking over her shoulder at him.

"Oh, there are other commanders? How many?"

Narra stopped mid step. Mika skidded to a stop behind her. He was inches away from her face when she spun on her heel to face him. She jabbed her finger into his sternum and glared up into his cold eyes. "Stop asking questions. This is none of your business."

"No, but it's fun to watch you squirm." Mika chuckled, his chest rumbling against her finger.

She quickly dropped her hand. "I know you're afraid I'll slip away and leave you high and dry, but you know where I damn well *live*. I'm not going anywhere. Not with all this mess going on. Not with Avalon still at my home, and not without making sure this war ends peacefully."

Mika raised an eyebrow, but his smirk finally twisted into a frown. "You have a lot to do."

"And yet here I am arguing with *you*." Narra placed her hands on her hips. "Stop delaying me."

The smile was back, but the amusement was missing from his eyes. "Fine, death bringer. I'll wait in the sewer while you wrangle your thieves."

Narra narrowed her eyes suspiciously. "You promise?"

His smirk grew. "I promise."

Narra sighed. She didn't question it. There was no point. She couldn't make Mika do anything any more than he could control her. She knew he was only tormenting her today because she hadn't kept her word yesterday. Though he had protected Avalon throughout the battle for the palace, she wouldn't help him locate her mother. He was sour about it, and he was taking it out on her in one of the worst ways possible.

Her patience was worn thin, but at least he seemed honest when he promised to stay in the sewer. She hoped he meant it.

Narra continued down the tunnel until they reached the entrance to the manor. She gave Mika a sideways glance, but he just winked and sunk into the shadows. Relief relaxed the tense muscles in her shoulders. She quickly climbed the ladder and pushed open the hatch.

Dull light flooded in from the basement, and she quickly leapt out into the cellar. Once she and Erik were both out of the sewer, they climbed the stairs into the manor.

The air was stale and the manor was quiet, aside from the howl of wind on the windows. She walked down the hall and her heartbeat sped up as she beelined to the parlor on the first floor.

"What's your plan?" Erik asked.

"We find the commanders. I'll hold a meeting, get them

on my side, and then we'll be set for tomorrow," Narra said quickly.

Erik snorted. "Sure."

He was right. Getting the commanders to work together and follow her directions was going to be a nightmare, but she'd prepared for this. Before Asher had disappeared last night, they'd made a plan. She only hoped it was enough.

Narra pushed the parlor door open and stepped inside. Her gaze landed on Graves, who was tipping back a pint of ale in front of the fireplace. He sat with his Boomers, a jovial smile on his face until he raised his eyes to see who'd barged in.

Graves paled and quickly stood up, sloshing golden liquid onto the carpet. "Rheka," he said. His eyes widened in surprise. "You're back already?" He didn't say it, but the question was clear. The war wasn't over, and here she was. What was going on?

"I'm calling a meeting. The commanders need to gather at once," Narra said. She tilted her chin up, daring him to defy her.

Graves blinked a few times before nodding. "Of course."

Narra nodded and spun on her heel. She trekked back into the hallway and up the steps to the second floor. When she opened the door to the meeting chamber, it was empty. She glanced around at the ornate furniture before walking over to the large window taking up most of the far wall.

Down the coast, she could see the sea warring with itself. The waves crashed and writhed, white tips flaring over one another—each wave consuming the next. The wind was strong today. It shook the trees and sent the windows trembling. There was a storm brewing, and it was not one of Avalon's making.

"Rheka, you're back," August said, sounding surprise.

She turned to find the elderly commander standing in the doorway, his white eyebrows furrowed and his moustache far thicker than she remembered.

"I am," Narra said. She glanced at Erik. He shouldn't be there. He wasn't a commander, but he was staying with her today. She needed someone to confirm what she was going to say was true.

August only nodded a polite greeting at her best friend before taking his usual seat. "I hope you haven't returned because of another ruined steambike."

Narra's cheeks heated even as a tiny smile pulled at her lips. "Your steambike is fine."

August chuckled. "I'm sure. I was only kidding." From the spark in his eyes, that was a lie. He really worried she'd destroyed another one of his inventions. "How is the war going? Does your return mean it's over?"

She shook her head. "No, but it has paused while we deal with a situation at the palace."

August raised his eyebrows. "I heard whispers that an army marched through the streets yesterday, but I haven't been out to see for myself."

Narra sighed. "I'll explain everything once the others have assembled."

They didn't have to wait long. Five minutes later, the entire Council of Commanders was seated, each giving Erik a confused look. Her best friend stood at the back of the room, close to the chair she had yet to sit in. He held his hands behind his back and stared down everyone to challenge him with their gaze. Clint and August were the only two that did not give him an irritated look in response.

"What is he doing here?" Klaus asked blandly.

"I'm allowing it," Narra said quickly. "The business I have today involves the entire Guild."

"Oh?" Claudia raised an eyebrow, her eyes flashing curiously.

Narra cleared her throat. "I'm sure many of you have heard there was a battle in Rova City yesterday." A few silent nods confirmed as much. "Former Empress Marina has taken back the castle. I was in the battle to retake it, along with General Asher Grayson and three platoons."

Graves' eyes widened in surprise. "Three? That must have been an easy win, then. There's no way Marina could have gathered enough forces to combat that in such a short amount of time."

Narra smiled ruefully. She'd thought the same. And it was true, Marina hadn't. If they'd only fought Marina and her mercenaries, they'd have won easily. But they hadn't expected Lady Death to make an appearance.

"You're right," Narra began, "but she had help... from Lady Death."

Each commander stared at her in stunned disbelief.

"What are you saying?" Claudia asked carefully.

"I know this is hard to believe, but Ashra is real. She's sided with Marina to take over the empire," Narra explained.

"You're mad," Klaus said.

"Hard to believe?" Claudia laughed. "That's impossible."

"This is a lot, even for you, Rheka," Graves said darkly.

Narra sighed through her nose. She stepped in front of her chair and braced her hands on the table. "I'm not lying. I wish I were. Whether you believe me or not, the empire needs our help."

Claudia snorted. "And what do you expect us to do against the supposed Goddess of Death?"

Klaus rolled his eyes. "I vote we remove Rheka from her position at once. The stress has clearly become too much."

Clint stood slowly, silencing them. "You should put more stock in what Rheka has to say." There was an edge to his usual monotone. The commanders stilled under his intense gaze, confusion filling their eyes. "Rheka should be dead right now."

Narra stiffened. That's right. Clint had returned from the warfront with them, but he'd had to head off and find Erik so that he could say his goodbyes. He'd returned briefly with her best friend but didn't stay long. He had probably thought she was dead and Erik was off grieving somewhere.

"What is that supposed to mean?" Claudia squawked.

"She was shot on the battlefield. She should have died." Clint's dark gaze met hers.

"That doesn't mean Lady Death was involved!" Klaus argued.

"I saw her for myself," Erik said. "She stood next to Marina at the top of the Imperial Palace's steps as ink dripped from her skirt and entered the minds of Rovan soldiers. She took over their minds and turned them against us. She *stole* the army for herself."

Everyone stared at Erik. Even Narra was surprised he'd spoken up.

"You're Rheka's friend," Klaus said after a long minute of silence. "Of course you'd defend her."

Erik rolled his eyes.

"Is this true, Rheka?" August asked reverently.

Narra nodded, her jaw set. "I'm afraid so."

August sat back hard. "I never thought I'd see the day."

"August, you can't be listening to this foolishness!" Klaus snapped.

"Why would she lie, Klaus? Why would Erik?" August challenged.

Klaus hesitated, his mouth hanging open, but no sound escaped.

Narra sighed. This was getting out of hand. "Whatever you believe, it doesn't matter. The crown is hiring the Thieves—all of them. Grayson wants the Guild to cause a huge distraction while the rest of us sneak inside the castle to end this."

"Distraction you say?" Graves asked, sounding excited. Sparks flashed through his eyes. Narra recognized that look. He knew he was going to get to blow something up.

"Yes," Narra said. "Do whatever you want. Blow shit up, create traps, incapacitate the enemy—whatever. I don't care as long as all eyes are outside the palace when we enter."

"This sounds like an expensive job," Clint said.

Narra smiled. "It is. Grayson will pay each faction five hundred gold coins to do it."

Every mouth in the room fell open but hers and Erik's. That was a *damn lot* of gold. That could feed the country for years. It could buy castles and armies—anything you could ever want. Even separated into five hundred each, it was enough to keep each faction of the Thieves Guild going for years and years to come.

"Am I dreaming?" Claudia asked. She blinked slowly, like she was coming out of sleep.

"No," Narra said. "This is real. The money is real. But I need this all to happen tomorrow. You have the day to prepare."

At the mention of their short time table, their eyebrows furrowed, and she could almost see the thoughts spinning through their minds. There was much to be done—calculations to be made. They had to wrangle their factions and coordinate with one another immediately.

"I suggest you get to work," Narra said. "Or you might just lose the real score of a lifetime."

Erik scoffed. He remembered the term the initiates had once used to describe the loot her father had apparently gotten away with. They said he'd gotten away with the score of a lifetime; only Quinn was dead, killed by his own brother.

"Do we have a deal?" Narra looked at each of the commanders.

Every one of them nodded except for Klaus.

"How do we know this isn't a trick?" he asked.

Narra sighed. "If it's a trick, don't do it and watch as your fellow thieves grow wealthy."

Klaus narrowed his eyes at her. He hated her logic, maybe just as much as he hated her in general. "All right."

Narra smiled and straightened, leaving her hands to fall back at her sides. "Excellent. The distraction must commence at dusk. No sooner, no later."

"Understood," August said. His fingers tapped the table, jittery with excitement.

"Have fun, Thieves," Narra said. "I'll see you all tomorrow."

Narra took the opportunity to leave, and Erik was quick on her heels. They hadn't even reached the stairs when she heard the commanders talking excitedly. Their voices permeated the door she'd shut, drifting down the hall and into the foyer. Soon, the entire Guild would know what was ahead of them.

"Narra!"

She turned at the familiar voice to find Alden walking down the hall. He glanced over her shoulder, his forehead wrinkling when he heard the commotion from the meeting room.

"What's going on?" Alden asked. "Is everything all right?" He gave her and Erik a quick once over, inspecting for injuries.

"We're fine," Narra said.

"But the empire isn't," Erik added.

Alden looked between them. He must have realized how grave the situation was because he nodded without questioning it and quickly motioned for them to follow. Alden led them upstairs to the same study she remembered sharing a drink with her family in. It was a fairly large room with a bar on one side and an enormous desk by the window. There was plenty of seating, which she'd shared with Alden, Khlara, and Erik only weeks ago—before her mother betrayed her.

"Tell me everything," Alden insisted.

Narra and Erik exchanged a look. Where to even begin?

Erik began explaining the war and what brought them back. When Alden heard of Narra's injury, he went to her side and took her hand.

"Niece, are you all right? How are you even standing with an injury like that?" Alden asked.

"Let him finish," Narra said gently. She looked back at Erik and nodded.

Her best friend continued, explaining how she'd healed and what had happened since. He didn't skip over the magic this time, or Ashra. Before the end of it, Narra had to lead her uncle into one of the plush armchairs before he collapsed.

Alden stared wide-eyed at the ground. He clutched his hair in his hands. "It's all true?"

"It is," Narra said. "I'm sorry you had to find out like this."

Alden chuckled darkly. "It's all right, Narra. I understand why you didn't tell me sooner. I don't think I would have believed it anyway."

And he hadn't, until she had showed him the scars peppering her belly where she'd been shot. No healer could have fixed her so quickly. It would have taken years for a normal wound to create raised white scars like that. Magic was the only answer.

"This is crazy," Alden continued.

"I know," Narra said.

"Well, it is kind of just our lives now," Erik joked.

Narra chuckled. He wasn't wrong.

"How long have you kids been dealing with this?" Alden looked between them.

"Kids? Really, old man?" Erik sighed and shook his head.

"Old man?" Alden flashed a small grin as he stood. "Come here and say that to my face."

"Thought I just did."

Then they were wrestling, and Narra rolled her eyes in exasperation. "Come on you two, this isn't the time."

Even as she said it, their actions warmed her heart. It had been so long since she'd seen the two of them act so easy going together. She couldn't wait for this all to be over so she could see more of it.

Erik breathed heavily as he broke away from her uncle. "All right, all right. We'll pick this up later."

Alden caught his breath before flashing them a smirk. "So, where are we heading?"

Narra and Erik exchanged a confused look. "We?"

Narra opened the door to her apartment to find the smell of chicken and baked potatoes drifting through her home. She tilted her chin up, sniffing the air to savor the scent. It had been a long time since someone had cooked her something other than breakfast.

She paused a few steps in, and the vault-door closed behind her and her three comrades with a *whoosh*. She tried to remember when the last time was that someone had gotten groceries, but she couldn't put her finger on it. There couldn't have been anything good in the apartment, so where had it come from?

Narra drifted over to the kitchen door where she spied Avalon's back. The pirate hummed cheerfully as she flipped chicken cutlets in a deep cast iron pan. Baked potatoes sat on a plate on the counter, steam rising from their surface. Her mouth watered, but before she could step inside, wrap her arms around Avalon, and beg to be fed, someone cleared their throat behind her.

She bit her tongue on a groan and reluctantly turned around. Asher leaned against the back of the couch, his arms crossed over his broad chest. He had returned with new clothes and a clean-shaven face. She had to admit that she missed the scruff, though without it, he appeared far younger.

"You're back," Narra said.

Asher nodded. "I am."

Now that her attention was off the food cooking in the other room, she glanced around the living room. Danicka sat cross-legged in the corner, her eyes closed and her hands resting gently on her knees. She looked like she was meditating, her chest rising and falling slowly as if she were asleep.

The other corner of the living room was empty. She blinked in surprise and stepped away from the kitchen to look for the pile of wood that had laid there the last couple of months. Ever since her father had smashed the table to bits during one of his drunk benders, the pile of wood had been a reminder of him.

Her chest panged, and she reached up to rub the spot. Her eyebrows furrowed with confusion. Was she sad that the mess was gone?

Mason appeared with a broom and dustpan in hand. He barely gave them a nod before marching over to the spot the woodpile had once been. He began sweeping the spot like she hadn't just lost the last remnants of her father.

"Narra?" Erik said slowly.

Narra swallowed the lump that had built in her throat.

She didn't know why she felt the way she did, and she didn't have time to dissect it. "Yes?" She peeled her eyes away from the corner and again looked around the room. It was so... crowded. Mika, Alden, and even Erik were still huddled near the doorway, seeming unsure where to go. Alden looked like he'd seen a ghost.

"You okay?" Erik asked.

She nodded. "It's strange having so many people here." It'd work as an excuse. Later, when they were alone, she might bring up the broken coffee table, but not now.

Erik looked around and nodded. "I don't think I've ever seen so many people in your apartment."

"I can't believe you allowed so many people in," Alden said. "What are you going to do when this is all over?"

"Get rid of it," Narra said without thinking. She couldn't very well stay there with so many people knowing where she lived. Any one of them could appear in the dead of night and slit her throat in her sleep. Not that she expected that from anyone but Mika, but the threat of it was enough.

"You've lived here all your life." Alden's eyebrows furrowed. He finally stepped out of the doorway, his eyes lingering on the same corner of the living room that she'd focused on.

"I know," she said softly.

Erik grinned, though the look was forced. "We'll find a new place. A better one. One with a secret, hidden room, and a back entrance. *Or* maybe one with rooftop access. It'd be nice not to have to scale escape ladders anymore."

Narra smiled. She knew he was trying to lighten the mood, and she appreciated the effort. "I'm not sure such a thing exists in Rova City," she said, knowing very well that her apartment had a secret room and a back exit. The only thing they were missing was the rooftop access.

"If it does, we'll find it," Erik assured her.

"Dinner is ready!" Avalon called in a singsong voice from the kitchen.

Narra spun around in time to catch Avalon's smile and the sway of her hips. The pirate placed a hand on her waist and winked at Narra before offering her a plate already loaded with dinner. Narra didn't hesitate in snatching it from Avalon's grasp. "Thank you," she said. Her cheeks heated as she gave Avalon a quick kiss on the cheek before sitting down at the small kitchen table.

"Avalon," Erik said in a mock-gasp. "I didn't know you were so... domestic!"

Avalon slammed her fist into his gut, and Erik doubled over gasping for air. "Call me domestic one more time. I dare you."

Erik laughed, even through his gasps for air.

When he said nothing else, Avalon grunted her approval, fetched her own plate, and sat down beside Narra. She crossed one leg over the other and gave Narra a satisfied smile. "Eat up!"

Narra chuckled as Erik slowly straightened. He winced and rubbed his stomach before slowly making his way over to the stack of plates and cutlery Avalon had left on the counter.

When they'd all gathered a plate of food, including Danicka, who Mason had fetched from her meditating, they sat or leaned in various parts of the kitchen. The room was full, with barely any space to walk through. Narra was suddenly all too aware of how many people knew where she lived. She would *definitely* be finding a new home after the war.

Narra groaned softly as savory chicken, flavored with an unfamiliar spice exploded on her tastebuds. “Thank Srah we met. This is amazing.”

“Why thank you,” Avalon said. “It’s been a while since I’ve cooked. Hopefully the cayenne isn’t too strong.”

“Is that the fiery taste in my mouth?” Alden asked. His face was red as he slowly chewed.

“Yep.” Avalon grinned at his discomfort.

“I like it,” Narra said. She took a few more bites as they all settled into silence. While they ate, Narra was too enraptured by the food to think of much else.

When they were done, Narra leaned back in her seat, a hand over her belly. She’d definitely eaten too much, but she regretted nothing. It was probably the last time in awhile that she’d eat so well.

“So, tomorrow is the day,” Asher said, interrupting the easy silence and filling it with tension.

Her once warm belly now felt heavy, cold dread wrapping around the food and making it hard and uncomfortable.

“It is,” Narra said slowly.

“We’re using your secret tunnel to gain entry?” Asher confirmed.

Narra glanced at the others. They weren’t supposed to know about the tunnel, but then again, they’d find out tomorrow. “Yes. We’ll take the tunnel into the servants’ quarters and work our way up through the castle to find Marina. Once she's killed, Ashra will have no need to stay any longer."

"And what if it comes down to a fight?" Danicka asked. Her wide, square jaw was tense, and her eyes were sharp.

"With Ashra?" Narra clarified, though she already knew the answer. Danicka nodded mutely. "Then we get out of there as fast as we can."

"Is there no way to kill or wound her?" Alden asked, sounding genuinely curious.

Danicka snorted. "You want to kill the Goddess of Death?"

"If she's leaking chaos like the assassin said, we might need to consider it," Asher said gruffly.

"If we leave her be, she might wither away by herself with no host," Narra reasoned. She wasn't sure how it worked, but if Ashra had done the ritual to seal herself to Marina, then did that negate the previous seal with Narra? She'd have to ask Ria more about it when she got the chance.

"We should be careful," Avalon said. "I doubt your goddess will let Marina die easily."

Narra hummed her agreement.

"We have no way of knowing exactly what will transpire with Ashra until we get there," Asher said. "But you're right, we should be careful, and we need to be prepared. Will the Thieves be ready in time?"

Narra nodded. "Yes. They'll launch their distraction at dusk."

"Good," Asher said. "I hope they're planning something big."

Narra, Erik, and Alden exchanged an amused glance.

"If I know Graves, he'll blow up as much as he can," Alden said with a grin.

Asher narrowed his eyes. "I don't want them destroying the entire city."

Narra shook her head. "They won't, but there will be damage."

"Better than leaving that witch on the throne," Erik grumbled under his breath.

They fell into silence once more. Everyone knew the plan. It was late, and they all needed sleep, so Narra stood and collected blankets from the linen closet while Erik and Alden helped Avalon clean up.

Narra returned a few moments later, handing blankets to everyone. When she got to Asher, he shook his head and held up a hand.

"I'm going to head home soon," Asher said. "We can meet at my home in the morning."

Narra nodded her agreement. That made sense. Asher's home was closest to the secret tunnel. "All right."

Everyone slowly separated for the night, seeming trapped in their own thoughts. The sullen faces of her friends and comrades disappeared as she headed to her room. Her body might not be tired, but her mind was exhausted from running a mile a minute.

The second she was inside with Avalon, she locked the door and stripped off her weapons.

"Keeping me in or them out?" Avalon joked. She raised an eyebrow at the door before looking back at Narra.

"Them out," Narra said. From the smirk on Avalon's lips,

Narra knew that the pirate was flirting, but she hadn't quite figured out how to respond to it yet. She'd never been a flirt with either sex.

"Good," Avalon purred. "That means I have you all to myself."

The pirate placed her hands on Narra's hips, her fingers kneading the fabric of the thief's shirt right along her hips. She gently tugged the cotton out of Narra's pants and began unbuckling her belt.

Narra's cheeks heated and her heart raced. "What are you doing?" she asked breathily.

"Helping you get ready for bed." Avalon batted her eyelashes innocently, though the smile on her face was anything but innocent.

Narra's mouth went dry as Avalon slowly pushed Narra's pants off her hips and then down her thighs before they finally wrapped around her ankles. Avalon helped her step out of them, leaving her legs bare and pimpled with goose-bumps. Cold air brushed her skin and she shivered.

Avalon took her hand and led her over to the bed. She pulled back the covers and motioned for Narra to climb inside. Narra did, her mind racing and her heart pounding with every bit of movement. Her heart felt lodged somewhere in her throat, leaving her barely any room to breathe.

As Narra lay down, Avalon climbed in after her. The pirate wrapped her arms around Narra and pulled her close until Narra was flush against her.

"Get some rest," Avalon said, breaking through the heat swirling inside her.

Narra blinked slowly. *Oh*. "We're just sleeping?"

Avalon chuckled softly, her warm breath brushing the back of Narra's neck. The pirate nuzzled closer and placed a soft kiss on her clothed shoulder. "Yes. There will be lots of time for... not sleeping when all of this is over."

Disappointment and relief warred inside of her. Narra may have never slept with a woman, but every ounce of her suddenly wanted to change that. Avalon's grip tightened on her waist, and her nose pressed against Narra's spine.

Narra closed her eyes and took a few deep breaths until her head stopped spinning and her body cooled. She snuggled back against Avalon, finding safety in the pirate's arms. She had never realized what it felt like to trust someone so deeply until now. She trusted Avalon with her heart and her body—two things she never thought she'd ever trust anyone with so fully.

Again, her body warmed, but this time it wasn't with an intense need—this time it was with gratitude. She slipped her fingers through Avalon's and squeezed her hand. The pirate returned her squeeze.

"Sleep," Avalon commanded softly.

Narra smiled. "Yes, ma'am."

Avalon chuckled softly, and Narra did everything in her power to ignore the bolt of heat that it sent through her.

THOUGH she desperately wanted to sleep wrapped up in Avalon's arms, the confines of darkness evaded her.

Narra sighed and shifted onto her back. Avalon's grip had softened long ago, and her breathing had evened out. Her arm fell loosely across Narra's stomach, the weight a gentle reminder of their encounter an hour or so ago.

Thoughts swirled through her head of the coming day. What would happen to the empire if they failed to defeat Marina? What would happen if Ashra got involved? She wanted desperately to tell Avalon to stay behind, but she couldn't imagine the pirate would agree.

She had to trust that Avalon could hold her own, but that was much easier to say when Avalon's face wasn't softened innocently in sleep.

Narra smiled as she stared at the cute parting of Avalon's lips. She watched the flutter of her eyelashes and the way black curls fell across her sharp cheekbone. Narra reached out and brushed the curls back behind Avalon's ear. The pirate's breath didn't even hitch. She was far beneath the surface of sleep now.

She turned back onto her side. No matter how many times she closed her eyes and tried to think of nothing, thoughts flooded her mind and kept her firmly awake. After another five minutes of tossing and turning, she got up. She couldn't stand it anymore.

Narra slipped on her pants, her boots and holstered a few daggers before clipping on her cloak. She climbed out her window and slid down the gutter to the street below. Once she had solid ground beneath her again, her breathing slowed. She circled the building and found the escape ladder. After a few leaps, she grabbed the lowest rung and yanked it down. It clanged loudly, and she winced.

She looked at either side of the alley and waited, listening for any signs someone was nearby. She heard nothing.

She sighed in relief and scaled the ladder, climbing all the way to the flat rooftop. The Criminal District spread out around her. The streets were mostly dark, but a few street-lamps remained lit in the distance, casting a warm glow on the brick walls of the surrounding buildings.

As always, she felt safer so high up. She sat on the edge of the roof and swung her legs over, letting them dangle precariously. She never had a fear of heights. Being above everyone else meant she could observe and wait for her moment. She could sail unseen over the city and reach places most normal people never would. The rooftops were her shadows. Her safety.

A clang from the escape ladder made her twist around. She yanked a dagger from her belt, her heart hammering against her ribs. *What now*?

Just as she went to leap to her feet, a familiar head of brown hair appeared at the edge of the building. She blinked in surprise as she met Asher's gaze.

"What are you doing here?" she blurted. Narra climbed to her feet and stepped off the thick stone rim of the rooftop. "I thought you went home."

Asher stepped off the ladder and straightened. He adjusted his coat. She wasn't sure if his cheeks were pink from the cold or from embarrassment, but they were bordering on red the longer she stared at him.

"I wasn't sure what to do. I kept walking towards home and then coming back." Asher sighed.

"Why?" Narra asked suspiciously.

Asher took a few steps closer so there wasn't an entire rooftop between them. "We never had the chance to finish our conversation. I've been trying to find the right moment, but you always slip away before I can catch you."

Narra shifted nervously. "Maybe I don't want to be caught."

Asher smiled. "You're like a bird that way. You always want more freedom than anyone wants to give."

She didn't like where this was going. Unease twisted her stomach the closer Asher came. When he finally stopped, leaving only a few scarce inches between them, she moved to step back. He grabbed her wrist before she could. His thumb rubbed her skin gently, making her relax against his familiar touch.

"I still think we can find a way for this to work out," Asher said. His eyes met and held hers, trapping her in his intense gaze. "After all we've been through, you must see it too. Even my soldiers have grown to accept you. Maybe the rest of Rova can too."

Narra blinked in surprise. She had thought she'd noticed the same thing. Even when his soldiers saw her face or hair, they didn't even blink at it anymore. They knew who she was, or at least that's what she had assumed. But was he right? Could the rest of Rova eventually accept her too?

Her stomach flipped. But more importantly, did she want them to? Did she want to be with Asher anymore?

She looked down, avoiding his eyes as she bit her lip. He pulled her forward, wrapping his arms around her waist. He didn't force her to look up at him. Instead, he let her think while wrapping her in his warmth.

She couldn't deny it. She still felt slivers of attraction for him. Every time he held her, or looked at her a certain way, she wanted to melt. But it felt more like her body's response than an emotional one. If he'd told her this, asked her to be his, even a couple of weeks ago, she might have crumbled. She might have said yes.

She cared for him in a very deep, very real way. But every time she thought about being with him again, her heart ached for someone else.

Narra gripped his forearms and slowly untangled herself from his arms. She took a deep breath, resolve settling within her. She looked up, finally meeting his eyes. "My first *no* should have been enough," she said softly.

Asher winced. "I'm sorry. I know I shouldn't keep asking, but I don't want to let you go."

Her lips twisted in a rueful smile. "You must." Asher stiffened. "I'm not yours to keep."

She wasn't anyone's to keep, but there was someone with a sultry smile and a delicious scent that she might allow to have a piece of her. Even at the thought, her heart pounded harder. It was the response Asher used to give her, but she couldn't find it within her any longer.

"Narra..." He reached for her elbow, but she took a step back.

"This is over," Narra said, putting as much finality into her voice as she could. "For good."

Asher's eyebrows furrowed as devastation took over his face. She couldn't bear to look at his pain, so she looked away. She breathed through her nose until she stopped the burning in the back of her eyes.

"I'll see you tomorrow." Narra walked around the general and back to the escape ladder. She couldn't breathe again until she reached the alley floor. Only there did she gasp for breath and hold her cloak tight to her chest. Part of her felt crushed, turned to dust and cast into the wind, while another part fluttered like wings.

It was a strange mix of loss and freedom. Coupled with her desire for a certain pirate, she quickly slipped around the building and scaled the gutter back to her bedroom window.

Narra slipped back into her bedroom and quickly stripped her outerwear off. As soon as her legs were exposed to the cold air, and her boots and cloak were in a pile on the floor, she stopped to take in Avalon's sleeping form.

Her heart pounded at the sight of the pirate. Avalon's bronze shoulder was exposed to the cold, and her dark curls spilled over the pillow. She nuzzled into her hand, her fingers twitching slightly on top of the sheets.

Narra's chest swelled and her breath caught. Suddenly tears burned the back of her eyes for the second time that night. She realized now that she couldn't bear to lose this woman. She couldn't imagine not having Avalon in her life anymore. She couldn't image losing her in battle tomorrow, or sometime in the future. She never wanted to be apart from Avalon's sly smile or sarcastic quirk of her eyebrow. She adored the pirate's stubborn attitude and wicked temper. She loved Avalon's hidden sweet side and the cunning look in her eyes when she planned. She loved the way Avalon cared so much for an orphan tiger and a daughter she'd never get to see again. She loved her pain and her joy, her heart and her soul.

She loved everything about this woman.

Narra blinked back tears again. She didn't just love everything about the pirate. She *loved* Avalon.

Avalon stirred, her fingers tensing on the sheets beside her. Her hand searched for a moment before she twisted to look for Narra. Her sleepy gaze met Narra's, and she blinked through the bleariness in her eyes.

"Narra?" Avalon asked, her voice husky with sleep. "What are you doing? Come back to bed."

Narra took a tentative step forward, then another. The revelation inside her was like a hot balloon, desperate to be popped and said aloud. But the words clung to her tongue and refused to be said.

Avalon pulled back the blanket and patted the bed beside her. Narra slowly slipped back in, settling on her side only a few inches away from Avalon. The pirate reached for her, trying to pull Narra back into her arms, but Narra stiffened.

Avalon slowly opened her eyes, her forehead wrinkling in confusion. "What's wrong?"

Narra stared into the dark depths of her eyes, flecked with splinters of gold. She reached out, cupping Avalon's cheek and rubbing her thumb along her cheekbone. "Tomorrow morning I want you to call your ship and sail away before things get worse."

Avalon jumped a little. The rest of the sleepy haze

clinging to her fell away, and her body grew as stiff as Narra's. "Why would you ask me that?"

Narra sighed. "I can't bear to see you hurt. What if something happened to you? What if you were killed?" Tears welled in her eyes and she blinked furiously, trying to hold them back.

Avalon's suspicious gaze softened, and she reached out to hold Narra's cheek in the same way. "Oh, Narra. What if something happened to *you*? What if I wasn't there to help you?"

Narra shook her head. "I'll be fine."

Avalon's grip tightened slightly and her voice dropped sternly. "And what if you're not? What if you're shot again, or worse?"

Narra's heart squeezed. "I'll be okay. I always get out alive."

"Until you don't. You always get out alive until you *don't*."

"*Please*," Narra begged. "Don't go tomorrow. Call your ship and get somewhere safe. I'll find you when this is all over."

"No," Avalon said.

Narra's heartbeat sped up. "Avalon."

"No," she insisted. "How can you even ask me this? I'm not going anywhere until I know you're safe."

Narra groaned. She was so stubborn. She loved and hated it at the same time. "What about your crew? What about Kaja? What happens to them if you don't return?"

Avalon scoffed. She removed her hand from Narra's cheek and gripped the back of her neck, forcing Narra's gaze to meet her own. "That was low, and you know it."

She winced. "I know." But she wasn't sorry. She'd try anything—say anything—to keep Avalon safe.

"I'm not going anywhere. I don't care what you say, how much you beg, or how hard you try to push me away. I know what you're doing, but I am *here* for you. If you can't keep us safe, *I* will." Avalon weaved her fingers through Narra's hair and pulled her closer.

Their lips crashed together. Heat coursed through her, making her gasp at the intensity of Avalon's kiss. Narra broke away quickly to take a breath, but Avalon continued to kiss her way down Narra's throat, making her moan.

Need swelled within her suddenly, and she took Avalon's hip in hand, pulling her closer until their legs intertwined.

"I'm not leaving you," Avalon said between kisses.

Narra pulled Avalon's face back up, kissing her fiercely. Avalon slid her tongue along Narra's lower lip, and Narra opened to allow her entrance. Their tongues warred with one another until Narra's need built so much she couldn't think anymore. She pressed her thighs together and trailed her hand up Avalon's hip, slipping it beneath her shirt and up her spine.

Avalon moaned into their kiss. Her breath was hot on Narra's face as the pirate slowly arched up onto her elbow, laying part of her curvy body on top of Narra's.

Narra's breath caught as Avalon slipped a leg over her, straddling her hips, and pressed her breasts against Narra's chest. "Avalon," Narra moaned. She wrapped her fingers in Avalon's hair and forced their lips together.

Avalon began slowly unbuttoning Narra's shirt, only leaving enough space between them for her fingers to work.

"I need you, Narra," she whispered feverishly against her lips.

Narra groaned at the words, her head falling back as Avalon's lips branded her throat and then her collarbone. "I love you."

Avalon froze. For a second, Narra's heart beat too hard, and her mind spun. What had she just said? This wasn't the time to confess her feelings. She hadn't even had time to process them yet, and she'd just blurted them out in the middle of... well... *this!*

Avalon leaned back so she sat on Narra's hips. Narra looked away shyly, squeezing Avalon's thighs as she waited for a response. She didn't need Avalon to say anything now, but she did hope for it.

"Narra." Avalon's voice broke slightly, forcing Narra's gaze back up to hers.

Her eyebrows furrowed at the sound in her voice. The pirate sounded close to crying. Why in Srah's name had she said anything? She didn't mean to make Avalon upset.

Narra reached up. "I'm sorry. I shouldn't have said anything. I—"

"I love you too," Avalon said. A smile broke across her face at the same time a tear dripped down her cheek. "I didn't think you felt the same way. I'd hoped but—"

Narra sat up slowly, holding onto Avalon's hips. The pirate wrapped her legs around Narra's waist, keeping herself firmly in Narra's lap. The thief wrapped her arms around Avalon and pulled her close. They fell into each other's arms, and suddenly Narra's own tears were free.

"I love you, Avalon," Narra said. "I don't want anything to happen to you."

Avalon squeezed her tightly. "Nothing will. We'll get through tomorrow. I promise."

Narra nodded against her chest. She buried her face in Avalon's hair and inhaled her strawberry scent. Tomorrow they would be back at war, but she'd be damned if she was going to let anything happen to Avalon.

Tension filled the air at breakfast the next day. After a fairly fitful sleep, Narra was on edge. She drummed her fingers on the table and glanced left and right at the tiniest of sounds.

Erik whistled jovially, forcing a chipper attitude as he scooped scrambled eggs onto everyone's plate.

Narra forced herself to pick up her fork and poke at the fluffy yellow bites of deliciousness. She ate a few quick mouthfuls, but they were tasteless.

Today marked possibly the final battle for the empire. If they couldn't kill Marina, the former empress might become the next Ashra. While they tried to end the life of Asher's niece, they had to somehow distract Lady Death. Their plan wasn't a good one, which let Narra know it was *definitely* one of her reckless plans. But somehow everyone was going along with it. No one questioned her, not even Asher.

They were going to run head first into the lion's den in

just a few hours. Anything could happen. They could all perish. They could be captured and tortured.

Or maybe they would win.

Narra looked at Avalon beneath her lashes, keeping a close eye on the pirate. Images of last night flew across her mind and her cheeks burned. She'd actually done it. She'd confessed her love to Avalon, something she never thought would ever happen. She'd never confessed to anyone before. She loved her uncle, and she loved Erik, but she loved them in a very different, very platonic way.

She felt nothing akin to familial love for Avalon. She still remembered the feel of the pirate's thighs straddling her own, and her lips hot on Narra's throat.

Heat flared through her. She tightened her thighs and quickly looked away from Avalon. She breathed in and out through her nose until the heat faded. She couldn't let herself get distracted today. She had to focus, not only for herself, but for all of them.

She wouldn't let anything happen to Avalon. She'd sooner die.

Narra scooped up a few more mouthfuls of tasteless eggs before settling back in her chair. Erik continued to whistle, while Alden gave him a dry look.

"What?" Erik asked with a grin when he caught Alden's gaze.

"Oh, nothing," Alden said. "You're just very off tune."

Erik mock-gasped, holding a hand over his heart. "My good sir, how dare you!"

Alden's lips twitched in amusement. Despite Erik's forced grins, his attitude did seem to lessen the tension in the air—

that is until a soft knock came from the front door of her apartment.

Narra shot to her feet first, a dagger already in hand.

"Who is that?" Danicka snapped.

"Are you expecting anyone?" Mason asked.

Everyone was on their feet in the next moment, hands clutching their weapons. Narra didn't answer. Instead, she circled the table and slipped out of the kitchen, down the hall to the front door.

Erik followed on her heels, sword drawn and lips cut into a stern line. Narra exchanged a quick look with her best friend. She wanted him to be ready. Srah only knew who was on the other side of that door.

Another soft knock came, and then Narra was throwing back the locks. When the final lock *clunked* out of place, she mouthed a countdown to Erik. He fell back into a ready stance. When Narra hit *three*, she swung the door open, and they both raised their arms to swing.

"Good morning," Ria said dryly.

Erik reared back while Narra froze, her arm in midair.

"Ria," Narra said. Her eyebrows shot up. "What are you doing here?"

Ria shrugged and stepped inside, easily leaning out of reach of Narra's blade. "I came to see what your plan is."

Narra holstered her weapon and quietly shut the door. When she turned around, Ria was inspecting the group crowded in the living room. She didn't even blink at their half-drawn weapons. Instead, after a quick inspection, she spun on her heel to face Narra. She raised an eyebrow, awaiting an answer.

"What do you mean?" Narra asked suspiciously. Ria might have told them about Ashra and her plans, but she still couldn't be sure who's side Ria was on.

Ria rolled her eyes. "You're going to kill Marina to stop Ashra, right?"

Narra stiffened. If Ria brought this information back to Ashra, they were done for. But from the bored look on Ria's face, she didn't look ready to run back to her mother and spill her guts. There was anger in the assassin's eyes. She wanted a fight.

"We are," Narra said.

"So, what's the plan?"

Narra exchanged a look with Erik. "Sneak inside the palace, find Marina, and kill her."

Ria sighed heavily. "*That's* what you call a plan?"

Narra winced. She'd just been thinking the same thing not long ago. "Yes."

"Then you'll need my help," Ria said. "You're going to get yourself killed, Sister."

Narra raised an eyebrow. Ria was still calling her sister? Even after everything they'd gone through? Maybe now more than ever it made sense. They did have a bond that surpassed normal friendship—not that she'd really call them friends.

"You're welcome to come," Narra said. "We could use all the help we can get."

Ria's lips twisted in a sly smile. "You are going up against the Goddess of Death after all. Ashra won't go down easy."

Narra shrugged. "As I'm sure you've come to realize, neither do I."

Ria snorted. "I had noticed that."

Narra stepped forward and offered Ria her forearm. The assassin glanced down at her hand before taking Narra's arm. They shook arms and then stepped back quickly. "Welcome to the team, Ria."

Ria chuckled. "Now let's figure out a way to *not* get ourselves killed."

JUST BEFORE DUSK, they picked up Asher on their way to the secret tunnel that'd lead them beneath Imperial Palace walls, directly into their enemy's domain. But before they entered the tunnel, they had to be sure that the distraction went off without a hitch.

While the others waited in an alley between buildings, Narra and Erik climbed up to the roof of a three-story apartment building. They stood on the flat roof and watched for the inevitable destruction that would begin.

Her heart raced with anticipation. Part of her wished she was out there with the Thieves. It'd be incredibly fun setting off explosions and leading packs of zombie-soldiers into intricate traps. The Guild was sure to have the time of their lives while the rest of them crept through the palace, hoping they wouldn't be killed at any moment.

The sun was dipping low behind the horizon, warm light disappearing behind the distant mountains. When the last remnants of sunlight disappeared, cold darkness began to set in. The world was cast in blue, but soon night would reign and explosions would rock the city.

"It's almost time," Erik said under his breath.

Narra nodded mutely. She was too nervous to speak. What if the Thieves decided to disobey her? What if their distraction wasn't enough?

Any number of things could happen tonight, and she prayed to whatever god was listening that they ended in her favor.

BOOM!

Fire split the growing darkness of the city, an explosion rocking every building around her. The roof trembled and she braced her legs to stay standing as she watched the massive explosion erupt at the edge of the city. It had to be near the Barracks on the eastern most edge. She wondered if the Thieves were being cheeky, getting rid of military outposts while they could.

A smile twisted her lips as another explosion brightened the pre-winter air. Black smoke rose from the Shopping District, right about where she thought Varek Square might be.

Another boom sent her ears ringing. It was much closer, maybe in East Gardens. As the trembling from the explosions died, shouts rang through the night. Lights flashed on in every apartment or house window in the surrounding buildings. Even from here, she could see guards racing along the top of the palace wall. The crack of the front gates opening warmed her belly.

Everything was going according to plan.

"Shall we go?" Erik asked.

Narra looked at her best friend to find the same excitement she felt reflected in his eyes. They both wanted to be out there, causing havoc with the rest of the Thieves Guild. Her chest twinged. She wished she could give him that, but he'd never leave her side while she ran into hell.

"Let's." Narra led the way back to the ladder and down to the alley floor.

The rest of their team looked at her anxiously, their eyes wide and some even wild. It was obvious they heard the explosions, but they didn't have the same propensity for danger that accompanied being part of the Guild. Even Mika and Ria looked a bit frazzled as they paced the alley.

"It's time to go," Narra said. "The distraction has begun."

Asher let out a sigh of relief. He nodded and slowly loosened his white-knuckled grip on his sword. "Lead the way, Rheka."

NARRA LED her comrades through the dark tunnel beneath the Imperial Palace walls. Her heartbeat sped as she glanced at every flickering shadow. Erik walked beside her, his lantern held out to the darkness.

Cold seeped through her cloak and into her skin, but even as she shivered, adrenaline began pumping through her veins, chasing away the chill in the air. She pushed every ounce of focus that she could into her movements and her senses. She listened for signs of danger, but none ever came.

They'd nearly reached the trapdoor when the ground shook. Dirt fell from the ceiling, peppering her hood and shoulders. She glanced up.

"Another explosion," Erik said. "The Guild must be enjoying themselves."

Narra smiled. "It sounds like it."

"Graves will owe you one for this." Erik chuckled. "You know how long he's waited for something on this scale."

Narra snorted. "I know, but contracts of this size only come around once in a lifetime."

"Then he better enjoy himself while he can," Erik said.

Narra grunted her agreement. After this, he'd probably never get another chance to blow up as much as his heart desired throughout Rova City. Still, so far it seemed most of the explosions hadn't directly impacted citizens, and she was glad he was leaving the city intact. Asher would never forgive her if they blew up half of Rova.

"Their attacks are getting further between," Mika said, his voice a deep monotone, like he was mimicking Clint.

"They are," Narra agreed. "They're luring out the soldiers, and giving them a dozen points to investigate. Splitting them up is smart."

"It is," Asher said, sounding suspicious. "Who did you say this Graves person was again?"

Narra and Erik exchanged a look. "No one you need to concern yourself with," she decided on. She wasn't about to give up her Guild members, and since Graves used to be part of the military, there was a chance that Asher knew him.

"Shh," Erik said softly. "We're nearly there."

As if on cue, the outline of the trapdoor appeared in the ceiling. A few steps led up to the entrance, and Narra shut her mouth the moment they were within sight of it. They'd been quiet enough, but she needed to stress silence from here on out.

"Keep quiet, and follow my lead," Narra instructed. She looked over her shoulder, waiting for everyone to nod before she climbed the steps.

She paused to listen, holding her breath to hear anyone that might be on the other side of the door. After a few moments, she gently eased the hatch up. The underside of the carpet blocked her line of sight at first, but once she'd raised it a foot or two over her head, she could make out the cold hearth and dim lighting.

Narra crept out of the tunnel and into the servants' room. It was hard to see with only the light of Erik's lantern to guide her way, but she surmised the room was empty.

"Clear," she whispered. She didn't wait for the others to join her. Instead, she went to listen at both doors, one leading to the hallway and the other to the servants' quarters. She heard nothing on either side of them, not even a snore.

Her eyebrows furrowed. Were the servants not inside? No matter how much she wanted to know, she resisted the urge to open the door. Instead, she returned to the door to the hall and gently eased it open.

The hallway was as dark as the room they stood in. Maybe Marina had dismissed the servants. Or perhaps they'd all been killed during the taking of the palace.

Narra went cold at the thought of it. Her heartbeat sped up and she breathed slowly to get herself under control. Now was *not* the time to freak out.

"Narra?" Erik whispered close to her shoulder.

She glanced back at him. Seeing the serious look on his face was like throwing cold water at her. There was no time to panic. She had people to take care of. If anything happened to them, she wasn't sure she could live with it.

"All clear," she said softly.

Erik gave a quick nod, and then she slipped into the empty corridor. Moments later, they were winding up the twisting servants' staircase to the second floor. She knew the passages well at this point, having taken them on more than a couple occasions.

When they'd picked Asher up from his home in East Gardens, they'd quickly went over where they'd search first. They'd begin with Marina's study and then her chambers. It'd be dangerous, but they could do it if they all stayed quiet and had a bit of luck on their sides.

They reached the second floor in time to hear the clang of armor in the hall. Narra froze and motioned everyone to keep silent. Her heart pounded hard as she listened to the march of what she thought was two guards. They moved quickly toward the grand staircase at the center of the floor.

Farther away she could make out the sounds of other guards moving about.

Narra cursed under her breath. There were so many of them still inside. She'd hoped the guards would all empty out, but she supposed it was foolish to think no one would remain to guard Marina.

She glanced back at her comrades crowding the staircase. There were nine of them including her. *Emperor's ancestors*, why was she letting so many tag along?

Once the guards passed by the stairwell, she turned

around, waving to get everyone's attention, or at least those she could see with the stairwell so tightly twisted.

"We need to split up," she whispered. "There are too many of us."

Ria pushed up a step, wedging herself closer to Erik than either of them would like. They scowled at each other for a brief moment before Ria met her gaze. "I'll go with the second group. We can communicate with our beads." Ria held up a handful of red beads, the silver moon dangling from her fist.

"Good idea," Narra said. "Grayson, go with Ria. You know the castle best." Asher nodded reluctantly. "Take Mason and the empress with you." She couldn't see Danicka from here, but she heard a scoff around the corner. "The rest of you, come with me."

That'd leave her with Avalon, Erik, Alden, and Mika. There was no way she was letting Avalon or her family out of her sight, and since she knew Mika wouldn't be left behind, she forced herself to include him in her plans. They might still be in larger groups than she'd like, but it'd be easier for them to cover a lot of ground.

"We'll head to the study," Asher said.

Narra nodded. "All right. We'll go to the royal wing, then."

"Keep your beads in hand," Ria said. "It'll be easier to hear me that way."

Narra unzipped the pocket on her thigh and quickly pulled the beads out. She wrapped them around her left hand and wrist, leaving her right ready to do the fighting. "Call me if anything happens." She met Ria's gaze with a stern look.

“I will,” Ria said. “The same goes for you.”

Narra agreed. She listened to the corridor for a few more moments before they slipped out and their groups quickly separated, heading in opposite directions.

She gave Asher’s group a long look over her shoulder, watching until the four of them disappeared around the corner in the direction of Marina’s study. She clenched her fists tightly, sending up a silent prayer for Srah to watch over them.

"Stay close," Narra said over her shoulder. She gave Avalon a stern look. She wouldn't be losing the pirate today, or any day if she could help it.

Avalon gave her a stubborn look but accompanied it with a sly smile. "Your wish is my command."

The heated tone of her voice made Narra blush. She quickly turned around and sucked in a few breaths of air. *Focus!* They didn't get far before she ushered them into another staircase. They wound up and up until they reached the third floor. The stairwell let out right into the royal wing, making it the perfect place to slip out and search for Marina.

Narra paused at the top of the steps and motioned for everyone to stay back while she checked it out. Avalon opened her mouth to protest, but Erik shook his head in her direction, silencing Avalon's words. The pirate narrowed her eyes at Narra as she turned and leaned towards the staircase entrance.

She peeked around the corner in one direction and then the other. There were two guards standing at the end of the hall with their spears crossed in front of one another. She remembered two guards being stationed there before. They'd have to take them out if they wanted to get down to Marina's room unseen.

Farther down the corridor, a set of guards stood in front of each of the five doorways. There were ten guards in the hall and two at the end. She stopped to listen for the marching of others but heard none. At least they only had this dozen to deal with.

Narra turned back around. She needed to tell them her plan, but they were far too close to the guards. She motioned them back until they were halfway down the staircase. Once she was reasonably sure they couldn't be heard, she crouched. The others mimicked her, pressing in as close as they could to hear her whispers.

"Down the left side of the hall there are five doors, a set of two guards at each. On the other side there are only two guarding the end of the corridor. We have to take them all down as fast and as quietly as possible." Narra raised her eyebrows. She met each of their gazes, hoping they understood how serious this was.

"Only twelve guards?" Mika scoffed. "That's nothing."

Narra couldn't help but smile. She was glad he was on their side. "With the five of us, it really is nothing," she agreed. "But even so, if one of them screams for help, we're done. If we cause too much noise, we're done. If one of them escapes, we're done."

"We get it," Alden said, flashing her a confident smile,

even as fear flashed in his gaze. The rest of them might be fighters, but Alden wasn't. She was sure he could pull his own in a regular fight, but a fight with trained guards? Probably not.

"You should stay back," Narra told him. "I don't want you to get hurt." He shouldn't even be here. She'd tried to convince him to stay at her apartment, just like she'd tried again to get Avalon to stay behind. Neither of them would hear of it.

Alden shook his head. "You're making me sound like a wimp, Niece."

"Alden," Erik warned. "She's right. You should hang back."

Her uncle and her best friend exchanged a look, a silent conversation passing between them. After a long minute had passed, Alden finally sighed and conceded. "Fine."

Narra smiled. Relief relaxed her shoulders. "Thank you."

Alden grunted something non-committal and avoided both of their gazes.

"All right. Erik, I want you to take out the two soldiers on the right side guarding the hall. You should be able to throw a knife into the back of their necks between their chest plate, shoulder armor, and helmets."

Erik nodded. "I can do that."

"Be as quick about it as you can," Narra continued before looking at Mika. "You're with me on the left side. I'll try and take out as many as I can with throwing knives, but if I'm being realistic, I'll only be able to down one or two before the rest are alerted."

"I'm with you, death bringer." Mika smirked.

Narra sighed. She didn't even bother reprimanding him for the nickname.

"What about me?" Avalon asked, a suspicious edge to her voice.

Narra gulped. "I know you won't stay behind—"

"You're damn right," Avalon muttered.

"*But* I need you to watch our backs. Keep an eye on my uncle. Watch out in case Erik needs any help, and let us know if you hear anyone coming."

Avalon opened her mouth to argue, but Narra cut her off with a shake of her head.

"*Please*, Avalon. I'm not asking you to sit out. I'm not asking you to stay behind. Just watch our backs and engage only if you need to. We need someone to keep an ear out for incoming enemies." Narra raised her eyebrows, trying to convey how much she meant that with her eyes.

Avalon's gaze softened slightly, but her jaw was still tight when she nodded. "All right."

Narra sighed in relief. "Okay. Does everyone understand their jobs?"

Her comrades nodded. Erik had already drawn two throwing knives, while Mika, Alden, and Avalon pulled out their swords.

Narra yanked three throwing knives from her belt before she straightened. "Don't do anything stupid," she warned them. "If you get into trouble, shout. If we're overwhelmed, *run*. Don't be a hero."

She narrowed her eyes at them. She knew them all well, except for Mika that is. If anyone was in danger, they wouldn't hesitate to jump into the fight. But in order to keep her head, she needed them to curve that impulse. She needed them alive and safe, or else none of this was going to work. She'd end up too distracted watching them instead of fighting. She could wind up getting killed, and that's the last thing they needed right now.

"Ready?" Erik asked. He met her gaze, adrenaline flashing in his eyes.

Narra nodded. "Ready."

Erik slipped into the lead, slowly leading them back up the steps to the third floor. He was quieter than she'd ever heard him. Usually he was her loud shadow, but maybe it was all just for show. He did enjoy messing with her.

When they finally reached the top of the stairs, she paused to take a steadying breath. Erik did the same. His fingers tightened around his knives.

Narra tugged gently on his sleeve to gain his attention. She made sure everyone's eyes were on her before she silently began to count down. *Three... two... one... now!*

Erik leapt into the hallway first. She watched the quick flick of his wrist, and then his knives were airborne. She didn't have time to see if they hit because in the next moment she was jumping out alongside Mika, her gaze trained in the other direction.

She threw two of her knives, aiming at the small space between the soldiers' shoulder armor and their helmets. The first two guards closest to her went down. The clang of their armor alerted the others, but Mika was already racing down the hallway.

As the guards turned their way, Narra threw her third knife. It sunk into a guard's eye socket. He fell moments before Mika made contact. The assassin leapt and slammed his boots into the chest of the dead man, forcing him back into his comrade.

The dead body toppled over the guard while Mika jumped off and sliced at his next opponent.

Narra ran swift on his heels. As blood sprayed the carpet, Mika twirled out of the way of the next guard, flashing out his sword to catch the man's exposed hip. She sailed past Mika and his opponent, her sword clanging against that of another guard before he cut through Mika.

Her heart pounded as she ground her teeth and pushed back on the blade. Another guard began circling, squinting at her like she was his prey. Just as he made a move to lunge at her, Narra dove to the side, and her opponent's sword cut through the neck of his own comrade. The guard's eyes widened before a knife *thunked* into his skull. He fell back just as Narra caught sight of Erik joining the fray.

An adrenaline fuelled grin pulled at the corners of her mouth. She leapt over the fallen bodies to face off against the next guard, whose eyes were wide as he froze to the spot. Narra slashed her sword into his gut before she spun around his side and cut through the calf of his comrade.

Erik cut through the neck of the man she'd toppled while Mika leapt at the last two.

"Watch out!" Avalon yelled.

Narra spun in time to raise her sword and block the attack of another guard. It was the one Mika had toppled with the body of another guard. She should have realized he might be able to slip out, even under the sizeable weight of his comrade.

She growled, the sound rumbling deep in her throat as she pushed back on his blade. She caught a flash of black curls over the man's shoulder, and then his eyes went wide and lifeless as he fell sideways on top of one of the other guards.

Avalon narrowed her eyes at the body and wiped her bloody blade on her pant leg before returning it to its sheath.

Narra couldn't help but grin at the protective look in Avalon's eyes. She stepped over the dead bodies and wound her hand behind Avalon's neck, giving her a scorching kiss before pulling back and dropping her hand.

Avalon blinked at her in surprise. "What was that for?"

Narra smiled slyly and shrugged. She turned to check on Mika and Erik, but they'd already downed the last guard. "It looks like we're in the clear."

"I'll fetch your uncle," Avalon said.

Narra nodded and couldn't help herself as she watched the sway of Avalon's hips. After a moment she shook herself and turned towards the door to Marina's chambers. "I'll search for Marina." She looked at Mika and Erik. "Can you start stowing the bodies in one of these rooms?"

She received two nods of approval before they slipped by her to open one of the other doors. They left it wide open and helped one another grab onto shoulders and feet, carrying the guards one by one into the dark room beyond the door.

While they went to work, Narra took a deep breath to ready herself. Then she opened Marina's door.

The room was dark. Not even the fireplace burned with life. She shivered at the cold in the air. It had been awhile since she'd been inside Marina's chambers. The last time, she'd killed two guards and stowed their bodies as well. They really needed to look into hiring guards that were better equipped.

Narra took a few steps around the furniture, scanning the spines of hardcover books before she opened the double doors to the bedchamber. Beyond, the room was just as dark and cold. She searched the room, the attached bathing chamber, and the closet. She even searched the armoire and beneath the bed before she returned to the hall.

Alden had begun helping Erik and Mika. They were almost finished stowing the bodies when cold slithered through her mind. She froze and closed her eyes, sensing Ria slipping into her mind.

Not here, Ria's words whispered through her. It was almost like she could hear the words in her ears, but she knew they hadn't been spoken aloud.

Narra squeezed the beads in her left hand. She thought of her anger, but the adrenaline must have been enough to warm the beads. That familiar tugging sensation pulled at her chest as her magic lit.

Not here either, Narra sent back the message, hoping Ria could understand her. She still wasn't incredibly used to the beads, but she was managing. *We'll check the throne room.*

There was a short pause before Ria slithered through her mind again. *We'll check dining hall.*

Narra opened her eyes. Avalon stared at her, raising a curious brow. Narra cleared her throat and let her hold on the beads relax. The warmth of magic disappeared, as did the feeling of Ria in her mind. "She's not here. Ria's team didn't find her either."

Avalon raised her eyebrows. "So that's what you were doing."

Narra smiled. She guessed it must look pretty strange to see her standing in the middle of the hall with her eyes closed. "Yes. We'll check the throne room next while Ria and the others check the dining hall."

"The throne room you say?" Erik asked as he returned from the room they were stowing the bodies in. "I imagine it'll look different from the last time we visited."

Avalon laughed. She quickly slapped a hand over her mouth to muffle the sound, but her shoulders still shook with the sound.

"I imagine so," Narra said. "I doubt they decorated for our arrival."

Erik grinned. "You never know."

Narra rolled her eyes. She scanned the rest of the hall to find all the bodies had been stowed. "Everything set?"

Mika and Alden slipped back into the corridor and closed the door softly behind them.

"Where to next?" Alden asked.

"The throne room." Narra walked back down the hall, heading back to the stairwell. Her heartbeat sped when she reached it and began the twisted descent. The last time she'd been in the palace throne room, she'd been forced to watch Marina's coronation. The time before that, Narra had killed the emperor.

The throne room was cursed. She only hoped they had better luck this time.

~

NARRA LED the way through twisting halls, pausing every time she heard so much as the rustle of curtains in the breeze. Her palms were sweaty and her heart felt like it might leap from her chest. All the tension building in her muscles was beginning to make her sore. She hated not knowing what lie around the next corner. She could be leading them to their deaths or to the salvation of the empire.

But she never knew until they turned the corner.

Voices drifted down the hall, freezing her mid step. Her heart pounded so loud, it nearly overpowered the voices. She held up a hand to stop the others, then held her index finger to her lips for silence. The quiet steps of her comrades stopped, and she slowly drifted down the hall to the large doors marking the entrance to the throne room. The gilded doors were like the large gates to the palace. They had the same pattern etched within them, stretching from the floor to the ceiling. They were opened slightly; one of the handles stuck halfway down.

Maybe luck *was* on their side.

Narra pressed her back against the door that was fully closed. She held her breath and fought to control the pounding of her heart.

"The explosions in the city could be anything," Ashra was saying. "Rioters looting shops, or military trying to cause a distraction so we let our guard down."

Marina sighed heavily, and Narra stilled at the sound. "I suppose you're right. It isn't necessarily *her*."

Narra blinked in surprise. Were they talking about her?

"Exactly," Ashra said. "Now that my Daughter knows it's us she's up against, she wouldn't dare come after me. There's no way to defeat me. Anything she did would only result in the deaths of her friends."

Narra inhaled sharply. She couldn't hold her breath any longer, and hearing Ashra speak was making her shake with nerves.

She glanced up to find the others staring at her. Narra nodded slowly, then raised her hand and clenched the beads tightly. She pulled from her fear and turned it into rage for the goddess that would dare use her worst enemy against her.

She's here, Narra sent the message when the tug of magic pulled at her insides.

Silence descended in the throne room. Narra's eyes flashed back open to meet those of her friends. She was about to mouth the same message to her comrades when the door next to her shot open, cracking off the wall. An impossibly strong hand clamped down on her bicep and yanked her inside.

Fear gripped her as she stared into the dark blue eyes of the Goddess of Death.

"Daughter, how good of you to join us," Ashra said. Her smile turned wicked as she pulled Narra behind her, down the carpet runner leading from the door to the raised platform on which the throne sat. "And you brought your friends too. How *sweet*."

Narra's heart pounded hard as she tried to rein in her emotions. What did she do now? How was she supposed to implement the plan with Ashra in the room?

Ashra cackled, having heard her thoughts. Lady Death released her arm about halfway across the room. She continued down the great hall until she walked up the steps and sat on the arm of the throne, directly beside Marina, who now sported the royal crown.

Narra had no idea what to do, especially with guards lining either side of the room. There had to be at least forty in total, twenty on each side of the large room. They stood stalk still, eyes black and unseeing. Narra was sure that with one wave of Ashra's hand, they would attack.

Narra and her friends might be able to take on a dozen of them, but forty? They were all going to die.

"Don't be so dramatic, Daughter." Ashra rolled her eyes. She flicked her black curls over her shoulder and crossed a leg over the other. "You are still mine."

"And my friends?" Narra said through her teeth.

Ashra's smile widened. Her gaze flicked up over Narra's head just as the other door to the throne room burst open. The rest of her team burst inside. Dammit. Why hadn't they stayed in the hallway? They should have waited for back up.

"Your friends," Ashra purred. She tilted her head like the lioness she was. "I haven't decided on what to do with them yet."

"Kill them," Marina growled. She stood, her dark red skirts swishing around her ankles. Her beautiful face contorted in rage as she narrowed her eyes at Narra. "Kill them for all this wretched thief has done to me."

Narra scoffed before she could help it. "All I've done to *you*?" She clenched her fists until they shook. "You forced me to kill for you not once but twice. None of this would have happened if it wasn't for *you*!" Her voice rose until she was shouting.

Her friends slowed their approach until they froze halfway between the door and Narra, who stood at the center of the large throne room.

Marina tilted her chin up to stare down her nose at

Narra. "Force you to kill? My, my, Narra, you do plenty of killing all on your own."

Narra took a furious step forward. Fire flared through every inch of her. "Not until *you*. I'd only ever killed two people before I met you!" Her heart pounded hard as she realized that wasn't quite true. She'd always thought she'd killed two people, but she'd only ever *really* killed Erik's father, since her mother was alive and all.

Ashra growled, and then she was on her feet too, black smoke drifting from beneath her skirts. "I thought I told you to *kill* that filthy woman!"

Cold fear shot through the rage threatening to consume her. She gulped back her retort and tried to push through her muddled thoughts. Before she could answer, Mika stood beside Narra.

"You asked her to kill her own mother?" he asked, sounding indignant, like he couldn't believe it.

"*I* am her only mother. Khlara Rheka is nothing but a traitorous whore with a lust for power," Ashra spat back. She barely glanced at Mika. Her anger sparked clouds of black beneath her skirts. They spread out through the back of the throne room, writhing around one another like living things.

Narra felt the burn of magic on her brain. She was getting used to the feeling and recognized it for what it was.

"Let my soldiers take care of them all, Mother. Let them kill her. She doesn't deserve your affection," Marina hissed. Her nostrils flared and her eyes burned with deep-seated hate.

Something sparked in Ashra's dark eyes. She took a step back, leaving Marina in the lead. "Fine. As you wish."

Narra looked back at her friends, desperately pleading with them to leave.

"Once all you care for is dead and your soul is broken, maybe then you'll listen to your Mother," Ashra said.

Erik, Avalon, and Alden narrowed their eyes at her. They weren't going anywhere.

Frustrated tears burned the back of her eyes. Narra ground her teeth as she turned back to face the Goddess of Death and the former Empress of Rova. "Please, don't hurt them. I'll do it. I'll find Khlara and end her."

Ashra laughed, tilting back her head and allowing her voice to echo in the large space. When she finally stopped and met Narra's gaze again, her eyes were as cold as ice. "It's far too late for that, Narra."

Narra took a step back at the same time the soldiers on either side of the room stepped forward. They marched in unison, one step after the other as they closed in on the carpet runner. She swung around at the same time she ripped her sword free. "Go!" she screamed. "Please!"

They didn't budge. Instead, her friends drew their weapons, perhaps sealing their fates.

"It's been lovely getting to know you, little death bringer," Mika said. None of his usual mockery was behind the words. He sounded resigned to death, like he'd given up.

Narra turned to face him. "Don't call me that."

Mika's lips twitched in a rueful smile. "Finish my contract for me, sweetheart, and I won't ever call you that again." He met her gaze.

Her retort froze on her lips as she spied the rest of their friends charging towards the throne room doors. "Emperor's ancestors!" she shouted the curse. Her fingers tightened on the hilt of her sword. She spun to face Lady Death and her sworn enemy.

Ashra smirked as she sat back on the arm of the throne. Marina remained standing, her eyes filled with blood lust.

"Don't let me down, assassin," Narra snapped. "There are forty of them and nine of us."

Mika scoffed. "I've had worse odds."

Narra shook her head in disbelief. She couldn't imagine worse odds than that.

Before she could say so, the soldiers were on them, forcing them back towards their friends as they closed ranks.

"Kill them all!" Marina cackled from somewhere behind the hoard of soldiers.

Narra's heartbeat sped as she raised her sword. The soldiers hadn't been attacking before then, but now they brandished their weapons and shot forward.

Her blade slammed against that of one of the zombie-soldiers, the sheer force of impact vibrating up her arms. She gritted her teeth as she pushed him back, yanking a dagger from her belt and shoving it into his gut. Before he'd even fallen, she'd spun out of the way of a second one. She sliced through his throat, then slid on her knee, using her momentum to sail between two soldiers and cut out the back of their knees. As they toppled to one knee, Mika cut their throats, then spun and threw a dagger at another man.

Narra leapt back to her feet and used her shoulder to throw her next opponent off balance. As he fell back into two of his comrades, Mika spun into a low crouch and whipped his heel out, taking the man's feet out from under him. Narra took her chance and drove her blade right through his eye before leaping away to stand back to back with the assassin.

"We make a good team," Mika panted.

"It's too bad we're going to die," Narra shot back.

"Don't be so sure of that, sweetheart!"

Mika spun around her right side at the same time she went the opposite direction. She slammed her boot into the gut of the man lunging for Mika, and he flew back. Narra cut through the next soldier in her way, finally creating a path to the rest of her warring friends.

Avalon grappled with a soldier, Erik at her back. Her heart leapt at the sight of them working together. They both exchanged a quick look before Avalon ducked out, and Erik forced his sword into the soldier's gut. Once he was taken care of, Avalon slid over Erik's back to fend off another soldier trying to attack him.

Someone slammed into her side, and she barely caught herself before falling. A soldier cut through her bicep, sending searing pain through her arm. She bit down on a cry of pain before knocking him back onto Mika's sword.

Another cut to the back of her leg had her spinning in a roundhouse kick. Her booted heel cracked against the side of the man's exposed skull, and he went down *hard*. Before she could check if he was dead or not, a metal gauntlet slammed against her back, and then another collided with her stomach.

Air exploded from her lungs as she was overwhelmed. She couldn't see Mika, or Avalon, or *anyone* anymore, only a sea of armor with the Rovan crest emblazoned at the heart.

Narra forced herself to unbuckle from where she'd

doubled over and rose to one knee. As another soldier reached for her, she buried her dagger to the hilt inside his gut. Spinning on her knee, she sliced through the calf of another soldier, barely registering his cry of pain before she cut through a different guard's knee. Then she was on her feet, using a man's body to block a barrage of attacks. She pushed the deadweight into her attacker, then silenced the pained cry of one of the men she'd downed. With three men buckled to one knee, she tossed knives into each of their eyes before spinning to face the man she'd thrown a body at.

He pulled free from his comrade and swung his sword at her. She leapt back, just out of reach. Someone's back slammed into hers, but it didn't knock her off-balance. She looked over her shoulder to find Asher behind her, his spine pressed against hers.

"Asher," she breathed out his name, surprised.

He repelled two opponents who must have been after her, not sparing her a glance as he cut through the enemy.

Narra returned her attention to the enemy. The man growled as he lunged at her, but she faked to the right, then lunged left, slicing through his stomach and spilling his guts on the floor.

"Alden!" Erik cried out. His voice echoed in the throne room. She was surprised she heard it at all over the sounds of battle.

Her heart leapt as she scanned the crowd. She breathed hard as she searched for her uncle. No, no, no! This is exactly what she'd been afraid of. She didn't want to lose anyone—especially not her family.

Finally, she saw Erik pulling her uncle's arm over his

shoulder. Alden limped alongside Erik, blinking slowly as if trying to come out of a haze. Erik pulled him off the makeshift battlefield, Danicka and Mason jumping in to protect their backs.

"Narra!" Asher snapped.

She turned in time to see his sword collide with another guard's. Asher nodded in the direction of the throne room doors to find more soldiers piling through. *Shit!*

"We've got to block those doors!" Mika shouted. He caught her gaze, his eyes wild.

"Go!" Narra yelled back.

Mika gave her a swift nod before slipping between soldiers towards the doors. She only had enough time to watch him cut through two opponents before she was jostled back into motion.

A soldier grabbed her ankle. He looked to have been dragging himself along the ground, a long line of blood behind him. He raised a dagger to stab her leg, but she kicked the blade from his hand.

"Won't you just die already?" she hissed. Narra kicked him onto his back and drove her sword into the center of his throat. He coughed and spluttered for only a second before his eyes went blank, the blackness disappearing from his blue eyes.

Her eyebrows furrowed. She'd forgotten they weren't truly fighting the enemy. They were fighting Rovans. Her heart clenched as she ground her teeth. How could Marina do this? She was forcing them to kill their own people!

Narra turned her hate-filled gaze on the former empress,

who stood smirking at the edge of the crowd with Ashra alongside her.

It was time Narra ended the bloodshed. If she could kill Marina, Ashra had no reason to be here.

Narra pushed between two soldiers, one fighting Asher and another running towards Avalon. She sliced through the latter's gut as she went, but she continued her charge.

Her blade was like an extension of herself as she pushed through soldier after soldier in her way.

Marina's amusement died when she realized what Narra was doing. The thief was headed right for her, and Marina knew it. The former empress backpedalled, heading diagonally towards the curtains at the back of the throne room.

Ashra didn't even glance at her protégé, only smirked at Narra the closer she came.

Narra's heart thundered in her ears as she broke through the last of Marina's soldiers to stand before Lady Death. She breathed hard as she met the goddess' eyes. If Marina didn't want to fight, then so be it. Maybe Narra could bring down the Goddess of Death herself.

Ashra laughed, her voice echoing. "You can try, my Daughter."

Narra narrowed her eyes at the challenge, and then she lunged.

Narra sliced at Ashra's throat, going right for the kill.

Ashra's eyes lit with amusement and her smile grew as she sidestepped Narra's attack with impossible speed.

"You want to fight, Daughter?" Ashra laughed. "Let's fight!"

A black blade materialized slowly in front of Ashra's outstretched hand, hovering in mid air until Ashra clasped it in her hand. A fevered light flashed in Ashra's gaze, unnerving Narra as she circled the Goddess of Death.

She knew how foolish this was, but what other choice did she have? Maybe she'd get lucky and kill the goddess, or maybe she'd just gain her friends enough time to finish off the rest of the soldiers and kill Marina too.

A knowing smile pulled at the corners of Ashra's lips, but Narra didn't allow it to fully form. She leapt at the goddess and sliced at her gut, blade, and chest, each attack quicker than the next.

If Ashra was fast, Narra had to be faster. She turned her mind blank as she threw herself into combat. She couldn't let herself ponder her moves. She had to rely on instinct and muscle memory. If she did anything else, Lady Death would see her moves coming. She had to be smart, or at least distracting enough to buy everyone some time.

Ashra laughed at Narra's attempt. Her smile grew with each passing second. Narra leapt left and right, throwing out her sword every chance she got. Ashra mostly dodged, her steps artful, even as Narra used her momentum to slide on her knees and swipe at Ashra's ankles.

Her heart leapt with hope as her blade sailed closer, but Ashra was out of reach again. The goddess held a hand to her chest, overcome by her laughter.

"Daughter, you are too much!" Ashra wiped amused tears from her eyes.

Fire burned through Narra to her fingertips. She despised being laughed at. She'd been mocked for many things throughout her life, but never for her abilities. She'd always been strong and cunning, but Ashra was other-worldly. How was she supposed to compete against that?

"You're not!" Ashra answered her thoughts. "You can't compete against a god!"

Narra ground her teeth as she leapt to the side, again swiping at Ashra. She didn't let up, following each of Ashra's retreating steps. Lady Death arched a brow and raised her sword a few times to meet Narra's blade, but each time Narra swiped to the side, metal *shinging* together as she tried to get the upper hand.

She pushed all thoughts from her head and simply acted. Attack, attack, *attack*! Ashra's smile never faded, and she laughed occasionally at Narra's attempts, but the thief blocked it all out.

Narra used her speed to her advantage, but each time she nearly hit, Ashra either stepped away just in time, or surprised the thief by meeting her blade. Frustration bubbled inside her, wanting to explode in a ferocious scream. She swallowed it down and kept up her barrages until Ashra leapt high, putting several feet of space between them.

Narra continued to run at the same time that Ashra glided across the floor. She threw one knife, then two, but each time Ashra sprung free. She needed something faster than a knife, and faster than a sword.

As she threw a fourth knife, her fingers wrapped around the gold-plated six-shot revolver on her belt. Before she could think about it, she flicked off the safety and raised the gun. She aimed and shot.

Ashra's laugh became wild with excitement. She leapt back and forth as Narra squeezed off shot after shot. She adjusted to each of Ashra's leaps, but Ashra was inhumanly fast.

With each explosion of sound, Ashra got closer and closer until Narra could almost feel her hot breath on her face.

It was Narra's turn to jump back this time, barely avoiding Ashra's sword.

"My turn!" Ashra said gleefully.

Narra's eyes widened as Ashra sliced at her stomach. The thief leapt back just in time, but Ashra didn't let up any more than Narra had. Lady Death shot forward, darkness billowing behind her as she cut again and again at Narra's body.

She could hardly track Ashra's movements, and she barely raised her blade in time to stop several deadly blows. She winced as pain speared the side of her leg, then her arm, then her thigh.

Narra leapt away. She had to get distance between them. She raised her gun to get off her last shot, but Ashra was faster. A manic grin spread on Lady Death's face as she slammed the flat side of her blade against Narra's hand.

It might not have cut, but the pain in her hand was startling enough for her to release her revolver. The gun clattered across the marble floor, sliding uselessly far away.

Narra made a leap for it anyways, rolling over her head. As she reached for the gun, Ashra grabbed her arm and threw her back.

Her spine collided hard with the ground, and she bounced once, then twice, rolling over her own head before she finally got her feet beneath her. She skidded to a stop, breathing hard through the pain.

"You're very good, Daughter," Ashra commented. "But you can't defeat a god."

"Just watch me!" Narra shot forward, racing towards the goddess.

She was suddenly aware of the quiet in the throne room. The

battle didn't rage as strong anymore. Mika must have gotten the doors closed. She faked a lunge to one side and twisted around into a roll, sailing behind the goddess. She went for a backstab, but Ashra was too fast. She'd already moved out of the way, but Narra got what she wanted—a look at the entire throne room.

The doors to the throne room shook as someone pounded on the other side. Mika fought two guards close to the doors, a wild look in his eyes. Erik and Avalon were back to fighting together against three guards. Asher took on two opponents of his own, fighting close beside Mason.

She spotted her uncle at the back of the room with Ria nearby. The assassin fought off the attackers coming for either her or Narra's uncle. Her heart warmed at the sight of Ria protecting her kin.

But there was one person missing. Where was Danicka?

The heat of magic burned across her brain suddenly, and she looked sideways to see Danicka with her Crown of Bones atop her head, and her bladed whip in hand. The woman growled ferociously as her whip spun around Marina's throat. The empress flicked her wrist back and the whip tightened enough that blood poured from her neck.

Marina's scream filled the throne room, and even Ashra turned to look. Shock registered in the goddess' eyes, but it was too late for even her to do anything.

With another flick of Danicka's wrist, she severed the head of the former empress. Marina's head fell in a tumble of brown curls and wide, shocked eyes.

A screech of rage fell from Ashra's lips, but Narra took her chance. With the goddess distracted, she leapt forward, her heart pounding as she dove to stab her sword right through Ashra's chest.

At the last second, the goddess spun, her eyes wide with fury. "I've had enough of this!" she screamed. Her eyes went black and darkness spilled from beneath her skirts.

Ashra raised a hand, slapping away Narra's extended blade. Her sword flew sideways like she'd been parried, but she didn't stop her momentum.

Narra grabbed the bone dagger still stuck in her belt. Putting all the force she could behind it, she slammed it to the hilt right through the center of Ashra's chest.

Shock registered in Lady Death's eyes. Her lips parted soundlessly, and Narra stared at the Goddess of Death with wide eyes. She couldn't believe she'd done it.

Ashra blinked slowly, pulling out of her shock. A thousand and one things seemed to fly through her eyes at once, and then a genuine smile slowly spread on her face.

"Oh, my Daughter," Ashra whispered. Tears welled in her eyes as she reached forward, smoothing her hand down Narra's cheek. "Congratulations on becoming the next Goddess of Death."

Narra gasped despite herself. That wasn't possible. What had she done?

"Seek out my sister. Srah will help you with the transition." Ashra continued like Narra wasn't about to seriously freak out.

The dark blue gaze of Lady Death slid away from Narra and sought another of her daughters across the room.

Ria stared at the goddess with rapt attention. Her mouth hung open and her eyes were wide like saucers.

"I'm sorry, Sister," Ashra said. Her voice was different. It wasn't dual-toned, deep, or husky like usual. Instead, it was slightly higher—sweet and sad. Tears slipped down her cheeks as her gaze slowly shifted back to Narra.

Black swathes like silk-like material unspooled from the goddess' body. They floated in the air, wavering like they were caught in a gentle breeze.

The thief was frozen to the spot as Ashra leaned closer, her swathes of darkness coming with her. They wrapped around Narra's body at the same time Ashra cupped her cheek and laid a gentle kiss on her forehead. "Good luck."

Her voice fell away with the rest of the world, and then there was only black.

Darkness pressed around her on all sides. There was neither here nor there, no up or down, only nothingness. She couldn't feel her body. It was like her mind drifted on clouds of black. She wasn't afraid, though she had a feeling she should be. Something awful had happened. *Many* awful things had happened. But when she tried to think of what they were, her mind grew fuzzy. Something warm called to her, pulling her back into the darkness—calling her to sleep.

But Narra didn't need sleep. She needed answers. So with every ounce of will she had left, she fought through the shadows and the haze. She fought until her mind was too exhausted to try any longer, and darkness took her.

Narra gasped back into wakefulness, a chill wrapping around her. She inhaled sharply again, her throat aching and her eyes flew wide. Bright, piercing light slammed into her retinas, and she cried out in pain as she blocked her eyes with her hands. It felt like she'd just stared into the sun for too long and was paying the price.

With every breath, her body quivered and ached. With every movement, it felt like her bones grated against one another. She groaned into her hands and flinched every time a sharp pain cut through the haze she'd awoken too.

Scents pushed in on her: sandalwood, strawberries, vanilla, cinnamon, something sharp like the sea, and pungent cleaning oil. They were just smells, but somehow they felt overwhelming. Ringing filled her ears and pounded in her head.

Sharp pains continued to stick her skin, and each time she shied away from them. She couldn't think, could hardly breathe, without being in complete agony.

Her mind spun too fast, and the world was disjointed with too many shapes, sounds, and smells. Every time she tried to lower her hands, light speared her eyes. It was like she'd gone blind, but instead of total darkness, everything was white.

Her heart pounded hard and the feeling was like nothing else. It ricocheted in her chest and slammed against her ribs. She rubbed her chest and squeezed her eyes shut. What was happening to her? Why couldn't she remember?

Slowly, like moving through thick molasses, her senses began to fade to a bearable level. When she could finally think, her mind was a mess. Thoughts flickered through her head that weren't her own. She felt like her mind had been invaded, like sharp pricks of *others* had jammed their way into her consciousness. Vaguely, she was aware that some pricks were different than others. Some were loud and jarring, while others tried to slip their way inside, showing her flashes of things she couldn't remember happening to her.

Suddenly a memory hit her. She remembered every bit of pain, every second of agony as she burned through her transformation. But she wasn't remembering something from *Narra's* mind, she was remembering something from someone else's. Someone familiar with a manic laugh and cold dark blue eyes.

She shivered violently. She tried to escape her mind for the real world, but even if she could see, it was just as jarring.

Narra opened her eyes to look into deep brown eyes with flecks of gold, amber, and orange. Avalon's eyebrows furrowed with worry, and her lips moved as she spoke, but the ringing in Narra's ears hadn't faded enough for other sounds to push in.

She blinked slowly, scanning Avalon's familiar face. In her mind, flashes of other faces pushed to the forefront—faces only familiar to the *others* inside her head, but not Narra. They were other beautiful Rupan women that her past selves had known.

Past selves? Narra's eyebrows furrowed. She slowly sat up; thankful the sore, achy feeling deep within her was settling. She looked around at the people kneeling, crouching, and standing around her. Each of them held similar looks of worry.

But when dark eyes met hers, framed by dark curls, Narra reached for the woman. The woman's forehead wrinkled, but she accepted Narra's outstretched hand and helped Narra to her feet.

Narra tilted her head, trying to push through all the thoughts assaulting her. Her eyelids fluttered and she suddenly felt lightheaded.

She closed her eyes as images and memories of people she'd never known or seen herself overwhelmed her. Three little girls with dark curly hair and big brown eyes chased each other through the snow. They hooted and laughed, flicking white powder at each other before descending into giggles. They rolled and rolled, covering themselves in white.

Then the three sisters were older. They huddled beneath the floorboards of their home, whimpering as large men stomped around the house. Determination filled her chest as she tightened a small body against her own. She kept her sister close, pressing the young girl's face against her shoulder so she didn't see the blood slipping through the cracks.

The image disappeared, and then they were older yet again. Narra faced the same dark-haired woman, who was dressed in all black. They circled each other again and again before leaping in to spar against one another.

As the memories slipped away, Narra was left staring at the same woman from the memories that she was sure weren't hers.

"How do I know you?" Narra asked softly.

Tears filled the woman's eyes and then promptly spilled down her cheeks. Somehow, Narra knew this was unusual for the woman. "I was your sister once. We grew up together until you were taken by darkness." Then in a voice only Narra could hear, she whispered, "I miss you, Mona."

Narra tilted her head. Mona. The name was familiar.

That's where the memories had come from. Mona was inside of her, wrapped up tightly in the confines of her mind. She had a feeling that if she plucked and pulled at the strings of Mona, they would unravel, spilling the secrets of her mind until they muddled with Narra's.

"I'm *your* sister too, Narra," the woman continued. "But a different kind of sister." A smile tugged at the corners of her lips. She took Narra's hands and squeezed. "We may not be blood, but you are still mine, and I am still yours. Now more than ever."

Narra blinked slowly. It was still difficult to sift through her mind and sort her thoughts, but when recognition slammed into her, it forced a gasp from her lips. "Ria!"

The assassin smiled, joy flickering in her gaze, and then her eyes rolled back into her head and she collapsed.

Ria collapsing was like diving naked into the snow. Pain coursed over every inch of her skin. Narra could *feel* what was happening to Ria. She could feel the pain at the same time she was assaulted with memories. Memories of girls dying over and over again as Ashra took on a new form. But not every girl died. If they were close to their goddess, they could be saved.

She didn't know exactly how she knew, but she felt it deep in her bones—the certainty that Ria didn't have to die. Narra could save her.

Narra fell to her knees beside the assassin. "Ria!" she cried. She blinked heavily, trying to push through her thoughts, and those of everyone else who seemed to now be occupying her mind.

Ria was dying. She was bound to Mona, or the Ashra version of Mona. She wasn't bound to Narra.

Narra hissed out a frustrated breath. She didn't have time

ror her muddled brain. She could feel Ria's essence slipping away. Cold dread sat heavy in her stomach as she leaned over the assassin. "Hold on, Ria!"

Voices sounded behind her, but they all spoke, or thought, too much at once. She couldn't tell the difference anymore and quickly threw up her hands. "Silence! I can't think!" Her heart pounded hard when they finally obeyed her.

Think, think, think, Narra! Frustration boiled and climbed up her throat. She wanted to scream again. Scream because of everything happening in her mind, and all the things she needed to concentrate on at once.

She closed her eyes and squeezed her fists, willing herself to think through the mud. There, in the darkness behind her eyelids, memories flickered.

Narra grabbed the beads wrapped around Ria's arm and sliced through them with her dagger. The beads fell from the string and spilled over the marble floor. Once even the moon had fallen from Ria's grasp, she used the knife to slice open her own palm.

"Narra!" someone gasped.

She pushed forward and sliced open Ria's palm before clasping them tightly together. "I invite you, Ria Snowborn, follower of Mona, to accept a new path as a partner of the Goddess of Death. If your heart and soul should so choose to accept, you will be granted all the life an immortal can give you." Narra stopped. Images and words flooded her mind describing all the things Mona-Ashra had forced Ria to agree to previously. She pushed them aside and inserted her own conditions. "I will never condemn you for your choices or force you to choose sides. You won't be bound to me as a Daughter, but as a Sister now and until the day I die." Her heart pounded hard as she squeezed Ria's hand, forcing their blood to mingle. "Choose, Sister, and live."

Ria's body arched off the ground, and she gasped loudly. She tilted her body sideways, coughing and spluttering in her attempt to suck in air.

"Ria," Narra cooed softly. She brushed back the curls from Ria's face. "You're alive, and you're safe." Warmth travelled down her arm and spilled from her fingertips. It felt like sparks travelling from her hand into Ria.

Ria's shaking stopped suddenly, and she opened her eyes slowly. "Mona?" she whispered.

Narra's heart clenched. "No. It's Narra."

Ria sighed. "You saved me."

"You weren't ready to die," Narra said. She felt the truth in that just as sure as she felt the former Ashras in her mind. They were growing distant now, not so loud as they had been before. The only *other* she could feel lurking close to the surface was Mona.

"No," Ria admitted as she slowly sat up. "I wasn't."

Narra smiled sadly. "Mona is still here."

Ria looked up, finally meeting Narra's eyes. She started, jumping back a few inches. Ria didn't say a word, even as Narra raised an eyebrow curiously. "Your eyes," she explained.

Narra blinked and slowly touched her lower lashes. "My eyes?"

Ria's lips pressed into a firm line. She glanced over Narra's head.

Warmth scorched Narra's back as she realized there were people watching her. She turned her head slowly to look over her shoulder. A few gasps met her ears and everyone met her gaze with wide eyes.

"What's happened?" Narra asked. She didn't have a mirror to see for herself. She needed them to tell her what was wrong.

Avalon kneeled beside her and took Narra's face in her hands. Relief was plain on her face but so were an uncertainty and a wariness Narra didn't expect from the pirate. "They're not the right shade of blue." When Narra's eyebrows furrowed, Avalon shook her head and sighed. "They're dark like a stormy sky."

"Oh." Narra couldn't think of anything to say. Somehow she knew they'd say that. The warm tickle of memories pushed forward, but this time she managed to push them away. She didn't want to get overwhelmed and lose herself again.

"You don't sound surprised," Avalon realized aloud.

"She has the memories of the other forms Ashra has taken before her," Ria explained. She stood slowly, wincing as she got her feet beneath her.

Avalon stared in shock at the assassin. "So you're saying... Narra *is* Ashra?"

Ria brushed off her knees before straightening. "Yes."

Even as Ria said it, Narra was both surprised and not. She knew it to be true, but she also wanted to deny it—throw away her truth and run away. She didn't *want* to be Ashra. She wanted to be Narra and nothing more.

What did this mean? How could she be both Narra and

Ashra at the same time? From what Ria had told her, Mona had disappeared inside of Ashra. But Narra still felt mostly like herself. There was *more*... a whole lot more inside her mind, and there was darkness lurking. There was someone chaotic inside who wanted to burst free and wreak havoc with wicked abandon. But these people weren't her. They were just... there. They could be smothered and controlled.

But would it always be like that? Could they come out and possess her like it seemed Ashra had done to Mona?

"Don't panic," Ria said quickly. "What did Ashra tell you right before she consumed you?"

Narra's mind raced to find the memory without getting trapped by those of the others. "Find Srah. She said Srah could help me with the transition."

Ria nodded and offered Narra her hand. Narra took it and the assassin pulled her to her feet. "Then we find Srah."

Narra's eyebrows furrowed. "We?"

Ria shrugged. "You're my sister. Now more than ever."

Narra blinked slowly. She was pretty sure she'd said or thought something similar, but with the others clouding her mind, she couldn't remember without sifting through a sea of foreign minds.

Ria stiffened suddenly, her eyes flying wide.

"What is it?" Narra reached for the assassin, an overwhelming need to protect her suddenly blossoming in her entire body.

"My sisters..." Ria trailed off. Again, tears welled in her eyes. "I can't feel any of them."

Narra gripped Ria's forearms. Slivers of memories pushed into her mind. She could tell it was Mona doing it, but she wasn't sure how she knew. "They're all dead. I'm sorry, Ria. They went with Mona." If the other Daughters had been close, Narra could have saved them just like she saved Ria.

Ria collapsed into Narra's arms, her entire body shaking. No sobs escaped her, though Narra could feel her shirt growing more and more damp with each passing second.

Narra's heart ached as she held the assassin. "I'm so sorry," she whispered. She didn't know what else to do or say.

No one said a word as Ria grieved for her fallen sisters. Narra held onto the assassin until the shaking stopped and her tears dried up. Only then did Narra slowly pull back to make sure Ria was okay.

The assassin avoided her eyes but nodded and whispered an assurance that she was all right. She stepped away and wiped her eyes, putting some distance between them while she got herself together.

"Narra," Avalon whispered.

She turned in time for Avalon to crush her in a flying hug. Her embrace was stronger than Narra ever remembered being held, but she didn't feel any pain, even if she was sure her ribs should whine in protest. Narra returned Avalon's embrace for a moment, then quickly pulled Avalon back enough for her to kiss.

After a quick kiss, Avalon pulled away this time, her eyes shining with unshed tears. "I'm so glad you're okay."

Narra smiled and kissed her softly before enveloping the pirate in her arms once again. They held onto each other, Narra burying her face against Avalon's hair until she heard groans.

Her eyebrows furrowed as she looked up. On the floor

several meters away, the few soldiers that hadn't been killed during the battle were waking up.

Asher rushed to their sides, his eyes wide as a relieved sigh flew from his lips. He crouched beside the first man to sit up. Narra inhaled sharply. It was Dom. She hadn't even seen him during the battle, but somehow he'd survived.

"Hey, it's okay, you're alive," Asher said. He helped Dom into a sitting position while simultaneously inspecting him for injury. When he spotted blood trickling from beneath his armor, he cursed and yanked off his cloak, tearing a long strip before wrapping it around his middle. "You're going to be okay."

Another groan interrupted him. It seemed Dom wasn't the only one alive. As more and more guards came to, Mason and Danicka joined Asher in soothing the men, but only after Danicka had removed and stowed her crown in her bag.

"What happened?" Dom sputtered. He held on to Asher's shoulder as the general tightened the fabric around his wound. Dom winced and dug his fingers in harder.

"It's a long story, but we have the palace again and Marina has been killed," Asher said quickly, not seeming as concerned about that fact as he was about Dom's health.

"Really?" Dom asked through heavy breaths.

Narra scanned the throne room. She'd been so muddled in her own thoughts that she hadn't even noticed the blood covering the floor or the state of her friends. She looked around until she spotted Marina's head lying a few feet from her body. She winced and quickly looked away.

She spotted Alden leaning against the far wall. His head

had lolled forward, and his hand was gripping his bleeding stomach.

"Uncle!" Narra pulled from Avalon's arms and raced across the room. Her heartbeat sped and adrenaline shot through her like flames. Suddenly she was across the room, quicker than she could blink. She didn't have time to think about her impossible speed. In the next moment, she was kneeling next to her uncle, her mind racing for what to do. "Uncle! Wake up!" She shook his shoulders without thinking, then winced at her own actions and felt for a pulse. His heart beat slowly against her fingers. "He's alive!"

Erik fell to his knees on Alden's other side. He quickly removed Alden's hands from his wound, cursed, and then yanked his cloak off. He pressed it to Alden's wound, gritting his teeth. "You're going to live, old man! Don't give up on us now!"

Alden spluttered to life, a laugh vibrating beneath her hands. "Old man?"

Erik sighed in relief. "Yes, old man! That's what you are! And you can't argue it until you're better."

Narra sat back on her heels, her racing heart slowing. "He needs a healer."

Erik met her eyes and started. He blinked in surprise, and it took her a moment to remember that her eyes weren't the same color anymore.

What else had changed? Was her skin dark and her hair black? She glanced down to check, but her fingers looked just as she remembered, though she could see the pores on her skin with sharp clarity. Narra checked her hair next, but it fell around her face in the same vivid orange it always did.

"I'm going for a healer!" Asher called to the rest of them. "Can you make yourselves scarce for awhile?" He paused at the entrance of the throne room.

Narra met his gaze and nodded swiftly. "Send a healer to your chambers."

Asher nodded. "I will." He gave her one last uneasy look before slipping into the hall.

"Are you sure it's safe to move him?" Erik asked. His knuckles had gone white overtop his cloak.

Narra nodded. "I think so."

"Can't you heal him, like Ria did for you?" Mika asked.

She looked up and was surprised to find a wary look on the assassin's face, as well as a bloody scratch on his cheek. Narra paused, about to pull forward the memories she was trying to hold back when Ria interrupted.

The assassin cleared her throat. "No. I could only heal Narra because of our link as Daughters of Ashra. As long as Lady Death's blood ran through our veins, we could heal one another."

"Can't you do the same thing for Alden, then?" Erik asked. His eyebrows furrowed. His blue eyes were growing desperate as Alden slackened against the wall again.

Narra looked at Ria. She didn't want to call on her memories if she didn't have to.

"No," Ria said. "She can only accept women into her fold."

Narra narrowed her eyes slightly but said nothing. She didn't feel the ring of truth behind Ria's words, but she also felt deep in her bones that Alden would be all right regardless. His pulse might not be as strong as usual, but he was going to live long enough for her and Erik to bug him into an early grave.

Erik nodded solemnly.

"Mika, can you help Erik carry my uncle?" Narra asked.

Mika nodded and went to Alden's other side. Both men hoisted her uncle to his feet. As soon as they did, Alden's eyes flashed back open and he groaned in pain. While they had him lifted, Narra wrapped Erik's cloak all the way around his midsection and quickly tied it off.

"You'll be relaxing in a nice warm bed soon," Narra said. "Hang on, old man."

Alden groaned. "Not you too."

Narra smiled. "What can I say? He's a bad influence."

Erik gave her a lopsided smile before he nodded for her to proceed.

Narra stepped away and turned to lead them all back to the royal wing.

As promised, a healer showed up to Asher's chambers not long after they arrived. Narra paced the length of the room as the healer went to work cleaning and stitching Alden's wound. It seemed the blade that pierced him hadn't hit any organs or major arteries. It was nothing short of a miracle.

Her heart pounded with each step, which quickened the longer she was made to wait. The scent of copper was thick in the air, not only from Alden's blood, but from the blood covering most of their clothes. She'd sustained a few injuries during her fights, but the wounds had closed with her... rebirth. She wasn't sure what else to call it, but that's what the people in her mind labelled it, so she accepted their judgement.

She could feel how true it was. She was reborn as Ashra, but she was still herself—still Narra. She could push down her past selves and almost ignore that anything had changed.

But when she looked around or breathed too deeply she could feel the changes. The world was sharper, more vivid. Every scent, if inhaled too deeply, filled her brain and threatened to consume her. Even her movements felt sharp, almost painful at times.

It would all take some getting used to.

"He should be fine," the healer told Erik. Her best friend nodded, his shoulders relaxing. "He was *very* lucky."

Erik grinned. "That's the Alden I know."

The healer shook his head and left instructions on how to care for the wound and when to get a healer should he regress. He also left herbs to crush into the wound, and others for Alden to take boiled in hot water like tea.

When the healer was gone, Narra felt more at ease. She sat down hard in one of the two armchairs in front of the fireplace. She stared into the dancing flames and tried to clear her mind of turmoil.

It wasn't easy, especially with the last few hours still ringing in her head.

The chair next to her squeaked slightly as Danicka sat in it. Her blue eyes, which had once been the same as Narra's, were clouded and her eyebrows were furrowed. The empress stared blatantly at Narra, a thousand questions rolling through her eyes.

"Are you going to just stare, or are you going to ask me something?" Narra asked when Danicka didn't speak for a full two minutes. She shifted uneasily, pulling her attention away from the fire to meet Danicka's gaze.

"Apologies," Danicka said softly. "I'm being rude, but... I just can't believe it."

Narra raised an eyebrow. "Can't believe what?"

Danicka scoffed. "Take your pick."

Narra snorted.

"Ashra is real, and now she is you. My sister is the Goddess of Death. You killed Ashra... but now you are her. I don't really understand what's happened," Danicka admitted. She was rambling, but it made Narra smile. She felt the same. They were both confused for all the right reasons.

"I think... Ashra has been doing this for a long time," Narra said slowly. She returned her gaze to the fire. "But I'm not entirely sure why."

Even as she thought it, flashes of color—memories—tried to push to the forefront. She squeezed her eyes shut and shook her head. She was too exhausted to deal with them now.

Danicka finally looked away from Narra and joined her in staring into the flames. "You're destroying everything I thought I knew."

"If it's any consolation, I'm not doing it on purpose."

Danicka smiled. "I don't think I can continue the war having learned all of this."

Narra looked at the empress in surprise. "What will you tell your people?"

Danicka shook her head. "Don't worry about that. I'll figure it out."

"You really do want peace," Narra realized aloud. "You don't want to rule Rova."

Danicka sighed. "I never wanted that anymore than I planned on ruling Kiznaiver to begin with." Narra said nothing. She didn't know what to say. They were both in difficult situations they'd never intended on being in. She felt Danicka's pain. "Do you think General Grayson will be open to negotiations?"

Narra looked at the empress. "I know it."

Danicka relaxed into the armchair. "Good."

"I'll help you," Narra continued. "We'll broker a peace agreement between our countries, and maybe we could even create some kind of allowance for Kiznai missionaries to come into Rova."

Danicka looked at her with wide eyes. "Really?"

"It's important to you. I'll do my best." Narra's chest squeezed. She didn't know where this newfound kinship was coming from. It wasn't just because they shared a father, she knew that much. Maybe it was because they were in similar circumstances, or because she respected the empress. Either way, she wanted to help Danicka as much as she could.

"You're a good woman," Danicka said with a smile.

Narra looked away from the empress. She wasn't sure she agreed with that, but she let it go. She was too tired to argue. A thought did occur to her then. How had all of this started? "What made you invade Rova in the first place?"

Danicka stiffened. Her smile fell, curling into an enraged scowl. "After attempting communication with your former empress for months and receiving nothing in return, I decided to send an emissary to make sure my messages were delivered personally. What I received back was my messenger's severed head in a box."

Narra stilled, cold flooding her limbs. "That's terrible."

Danicka hummed her agreement. "It was a symbol of war. I couldn't let it stand or go unpunished."

"That's why even after Marina was dethroned, you still attacked."

Danicka nodded. "Our honor had been defiled. There was no other course of action."

"What a stupid woman she was," Narra said, meaning Marina.

Danicka snorted. She opened her mouth to agree when Ria cleared her throat. She slid between their two armchairs, an apologetic look on her face.

"Empress Danicka?" Ria said.

The empress blinked in surprise. "Yes?"

"My apologies for your emissary," Ria began. She twisted her fingers together, fidgeting from foot to foot. "One of the Daughters was ordered to stop your emissary and send back his head. Ashra wanted us to incite chaos for her to feed on."

Danicka's mouth dropped open. Clearly, Ashra's plan had worked. After another stunned moment, Danicka snapped her lips shut and looked away from the assassin. She clenched her fists in her lap, clearly upset.

Ria took that as a sign to go, and she quickly slipped away to leave them in silence.

Narra watched the empress for a few more moments before returning her own gaze to the fireplace. The wood inside cracked, and sparks flew into the air. She hated that Ashra had done this to their countries. She'd started a war, and now she'd left them to pick up the pieces. At least Danicka was open to negotiations.

All the same, Ashra was a part of her now, and she felt that chaotic energy lying within her. Her heartbeat sped up as if that energy felt her probing. It swirled to life, wanting to be used, but she quickly stomped it back down.

Ashra's words echoed in her mind, the ones she'd spoken right before Narra had blacked out. Narra needed to find Srah and figure out what the hell this all meant. She didn't want to use Ashra's energy, and she desperately didn't want to hurt anyone. If that meant she had to learn to control it, then she would—no matter how much she simply wanted to separate herself from it.

She felt it deep inside her that there was no pushing out Ashra or the others. She'd never be able to break apart from them unless death consumed her.

Narra looked up as she felt eyes burning the side of her face. She met Avalon's intense gaze. The pirate looked worried. Her eyebrows were turned down and her dark eyes were clouded.

Narra's heart leapt as she had a sudden realization. She might have been reborn as Ashra, but she was still Narra. She still felt heat inside her chest every time she looked at Avalon. She still loved her.

Her lips quirked in a small smile. Avalon's face relaxed somewhat and a smile twisted her own lips.

It was time for Narra to go. She couldn't stay here being what she was now. So the first moment she got alone with the pirate, she'd ask Avalon for a favor. She'd ask the pirate to sail away with her to the Wells in search of Srah.

Whatever else happened, happened, but Narra wasn't going anywhere without Avalon by her side.

Narra snapped up, blinking out of sleep as the outer door to Asher's chambers clicked open. The noise hadn't been loud, but it startled her nonetheless. Her heartbeat slowed as she glanced around his bedchambers. Alden was still sleeping soundly with Erik in the armchair next to the bed. Danicka was speaking with Mason in a hushed voice next to the window, while Mika stared at Narra from across the room. Avalon was the only other person who seemed to have fallen asleep. She sat in the armchair next to Narra, her head lolled back against the plush chair.

As voices sounded in the council chamber outside, Avalon's dark eyes blinked open and met Narra's.

"I think the council has arrived," Narra said softly.

Avalon nodded and slowly sat up. She ran her hands through her curly hair and straightened her twisted clothes.

Narra smiled as she stood and walked around the small sitting area to open the bedchamber doors.

Asher stood at the head of the table, looking over his shoulder at her. Dom, Sarin, and Lasar were present, grave looks on their faces. Their shoulders stiffened when she opened the door, and they regarded her with strange looks.

"I see you're assembling the council," Narra said.

Asher nodded slowly. "This is everyone."

Narra looked at the three familiar faces of the councilmembers, then back at Asher. "Gabriel?"

"Dead," Asher said.

Her heart constricted unexpectedly, but not for the general. Therin's emotionless face when she'd killed him flashed before her eyes. She swallowed the lump in her throat as she stepped in to stand by Asher's side, leaving the bedchamber doors wide open.

"So is Therin," Narra said.

Asher sighed heavily. "I know. We found his body in the courtyard."

Narra shook her head, her voice caught in her throat.

The councilmembers peered inside at the people crowding Asher's chambers. Danicka and Mason strode across the room to join them, as did Avalon, while Erik, Mika, and Alden remained where they were.

"You have... much company this evening, Your Majesty," Sarin commented dryly.

Asher grunted his agreement. His gaze was glued to the empress as she walked into the council chambers and stood on the empty side of the table with her guard.

"It's time to talk peace," Danicka said. She tilted her chin up slightly, an authoritative look about her.

Asher's eyebrows rose. "Oh?"

"I want to draw up an agreement at once so I can return to my people and stop this war," Danicka continued. Her gaze flicked to Narra, imploring her to join in.

"I promised to help her with negotiations," Narra said. "She wants peace as much as we do."

Asher narrowed his eyes at Narra, but nodded for them to continue. Narra and Danicka quickly explained what had gone on to start the war, including the Daughters involvement. No one argued when they mentioned the Goddess of Death. Not even Lasar and Sarin, whose gazes both darkened at the very mention. It seemed they'd both been taken by the goddess, having their minds controlled to fight against their own soldiers. They looked disgusted by it all, and Narra was sure they'd killed many of their own men. Nothing else could explain the fury in their eyes.

"It's been a long couple of days," Asher said. "Why don't we all sit down to discuss this?"

The others agreed. Between Narra, Asher, and Lasar, they carried in enough chairs from an attached dining room she hadn't been aware of. Once they were all seated, some of the tension in the room lessened.

"I want no more war between us," Danicka began. "We will pay for the damage we caused to the wall between our countries and send reparations for the... other damage we've caused."

Narra's lips pressed into a firm line. She knew what

Danicka was getting at. She'd send reparations for all the dead.

Asher nodded stiffly. "And? What do you *want*?"

Danicka smiled. "You're smart. I do want something. I want *true* peace. I want your people to understand our culture, and I want to understand yours."

Asher raised an eyebrow, imploring her to continue.

"I want to arrange for missionaries to enter your country and educate Rovans on our culture and our religion. Hopefully, as a result we can remove some of the leftover prejudice your people have against us." Danicka folded her hands in her lap and raised her chin in a regal fashion.

No matter how much Danicka hadn't wanted the position of empress, Narra had a feeling she was born for it. The way she spoke and moved held authority, but she never looked down on anyone. She had a regal air about her, but she wasn't beyond reason. Narra smiled. She liked her.

"After all you've put us through, you really think missionaries will be accepted by our people?" Lasar snapped. His fists clenched atop the table.

"I don't expect them to be accepted right away," Danicka said smoothly. "But I'm hoping you will help with the transition." She looked pointedly at Asher. "Maybe you could provide them with a space to teach and a small security detail to protect them, unless you're all right with us providing our own security."

Asher sighed. "It'd probably go over better if I assigned some guards myself. I could arrange for them to teach at the university and the palace. We could have rooms prepared for some to stay in Rova City."

Danicka smiled, a large genuine, relieved smile. "I love that idea."

Asher blinked in surprise at the stunning smile Danicka had laid on him. He flushed, seeming at a loss for words.

"What about the rest of Rova?" Sarin asked, sounding curious.

Danicka turned her smile on Sarin. "I'm certain we can provide transportations for a few travelling missionaries."

"And how would these missionaries gain entry to our country?" Lasar asked coldly.

"The Kiznai will already be reconstructing the wall," Narra said. "Why not have a gate installed with locks on both sides?"

Asher raised his eyebrows. "That's a good idea."

"I think so too," Danicka agreed. "When we're ready, we can meet at the wall and open the gates together. No one side will hold all the power. We must act together for our people to enter one another's countries."

"Maybe one day we could create a rail system between us," Sarin suggested.

Lasar scoffed. "That's getting a little ahead of ourselves, don't you think?"

Danicka shook her head. "That's a brilliant idea. I truly believe we will one day get there."

Asher smiled. "If you're as open to peace as I believe you are, I think we can too."

Their conversation turned back to a peace treaty, and after going over several points that needed to be included, they agreed to meet in a few days time at the warfront to make final arrangements and sign the contract. Both agreed to withdraw their army by the end of the week, and then the leaders of the two largest countries in the known world were shaking hands across the table.

"I look forward to our meeting," Danicka said.

"As do I," Asher said, flashing her a large smile of his own.

Danicka released his hand and stepped away from the table. Asher had agreed to supply the empress and her guard with a steamwagon to get them back to the warfront as quickly as possible. As Dom led the pair to the door, Danicka stopped and looked over her shoulder.

Narra walked around the table to say goodbye. Her heart clenched and her lips pressed together firmly.

"I know we never got to find out what being sisters means to either of us, but I hope we can figure it out one day," Danicka said. She raised her hand, offering her arm for Narra to shake.

Narra took it, squeezing Danicka's forearm firmly. "When I've figured this all out, I promise I'll find you."

Danicka smiled. "I look forward to it."

Dom opened the door and Danicka released Narra's arm. The Kiznai stepped into the corridor and Danicka gave Narra a small nod goodbye before they disappeared down the hall.

With the empress and her comrade gone, exhaustion began to lay thick on her mind once again. It had been a trying day, and she had a feeling she'd sleep for a long time once she was allowed.

"I think it's time we leave for the night," Narra said. She looked up to meet Asher's gaze.

The general met her eyes, his eyebrows furrowed. He

regarded her like a stranger, no recognition in his dark eyes. He nodded slowly and stood aside to let her return to his bedchambers.

Narra and her friends gathered their things and her uncle, who had woken at some point during their meeting. They sent for a stretcher to carry him home, and Narra led the way back to the outer door.

Asher had the halls outside cleared, leaving her an open path to the secret tunnel below the castle. A knowing look flashed in his eyes as she paused by the door, letting the others go on without her.

"Goodnight, Grayson," she said.

Asher nodded. "Goodnight, Rheka. And thank you... for everything."

She smiled. They had been through so much together. She had no idea what they were to each other now, but all she could give him was her friendship. He'd have her loyalty, and a small piece of her heart forever, but now it was time for her to go—not just from the castle, but from all of Rova. She had no idea when she'd see him again, but she knew the next time would be to say goodbye.

Narra sat down at the kitchen table in her apartment, a cup of tea in hand. She hardly felt the heat against her palms. The weight of her decision lay heavy on her mind. She didn't know how anyone would react. Would they be angry? Upset? Would they call her selfish and awful, or would they accept her decision?

She sighed and closed her eyes. No one spoke. Avalon and Erik sat beside her while Mika sat across from her. Alden was resting in her father's room, despite his protests that he was fine.

When she couldn't handle the silence anymore, she finally got up the nerve to ask. "Avalon, can I speak with you in private?"

Avalon raised an eyebrow, curiosity in her eyes. "Anytime, any place." She winked suggestively, making Erik grin and Mika roll his eyes.

Narra smiled and shook her head. She stood and took

Avalon's hand, gently tugging the pirate after her until they were alone in Narra's room. Once she shut the door behind her, Avalon's sly smile was replaced with a worry line between her eyebrows.

Narra brought the pirate to the bed and sat them down beside one another. "I have something to ask you. I don't want you to feel pressured to say yes in any way, so if you don't want to do this, *please* say so."

Avalon's breathing quickened and her palms grew sweaty against Narra's hands. She squeezed the thief's fingers tightly and worried her lip with her teeth. "Narra, you're scaring me."

Narra sighed and shook her head. "Apologies, I'm not trying to."

"Then out with it already."

Narra smiled at the command in her voice. Avalon was possibly the only person who could speak to her like that. She looked up to meet Avalon's eyes. "Ashra told me to find Srah, and I think that's what I have to do. I don't want to end up like Ashra. I need to learn what this all means."

Avalon said nothing as her eyes widened and her fingers shook.

Narra squeezed her hands. "Will you come with me to figure this out?"

Avalon stared at her dumbfounded for a long minute. When her mind finally seemed to catch up with her, she blinked slowly. A wicked smile worked its way up her lips. "I thought you were going to leave me behind."

Narra's heart leapt and her gut twisted. Every part of her revolted against the idea. "Never."

A tear fell from Avalon's eye and Narra reached up to brush it away. Avalon took her wrist and kissed the palm of her hand. "Of course I'll go with you." She kissed Narra's wrist before releasing it and folding her into her arms.

Narra's entire body relaxed with intense relief. She'd been afraid Avalon would say no, that she wouldn't want to go with her. She couldn't bear the thought of leaving Avalon behind, or going off on her own.

Slowly, Avalon pulled back, holding Narra's cheeks in her hands. "When do we leave?"

Narra gulped the lump in her throat. "Two days. I need time to say goodbye."

Avalon's excitement faded. Her forehead wrinkled and her lips twisted sadly. "I'm sorry, Narra. I know this is hard."

Narra nodded mutely, even as Avalon kissed her gently.

"I'll send for my ship and give you and Erik some privacy."

"Thank you." Narra kissed Avalon hard before embracing her quickly.

"Anything for you," Avalon whispered against her hair. She pecked Narra on the forehead before standing and disappearing out of Narra's bedroom.

Though a large weight had lifted from Narra's shoulders, this wasn't over yet. Her first goodbye would be the hardest. She had to remember this wasn't forever. It was only for now.

While she still had the nerve, Narra stood and returned to the kitchen. She was surprised to find Alden sitting at the table, glaring daggers at her best friend over a cup of tea.

"You're awake," Narra said. Well, this would make for one less separate goodbye.

"I am," Alden said. "Despite our friend here trying to force me back to bed."

Narra smiled at the scowl on Erik's face. "Let him stay up for a little longer."

Erik narrowed his eyes at her but didn't argue.

Narra sat between them, her heart pounding in her chest. "Mika, would you give us a little privacy?"

Mika raised an eyebrow, suspicion and curiosity flashing in his eyes. After a long moment of deliberation he nodded and stood. He must have figured there was nowhere for her to go as long as she was inside and he stayed nearby. He left without argument, the front door closing softly behind him.

The second he was gone, her family regarded her with strange looks. They had to know she was up to something. There was no point in trying to get them alone otherwise.

Narra took a deep breath. She just had to rip off the bandaid. "I'm leaving." She held her breath and waited with stiff shoulders. She expected shouts, maybe one of them to storm out, or slam their fists on the table, but they just stared at her with confusion furrowing their brows.

"Where are you going?" Alden asked.

"What do you mean you're leaving?" Erik glared between thick lashes.

Narra swallowed. "I have to figure out what's going, and how to keep from turning into Ashra. I don't know how long I'll be gone for, but it might be for quite some time."

Both of their eyes widened. Her heartbeat continued to thunder, her nerves souring her stomach. She looked between them, waiting for one of them to explode.

"Fine. I'm going with you," Erik said.

Her heart dropped. That was the last thing she wanted him to say. "You can't."

Erik growled. "If you think you're going—"

Narra stopped his tirade with a pleading look. "It's not forever, Erik. I *will* return. But I can't do this unless you stay. I need you to watch over the Guild. I need you to be the next Guild Master."

Erik inhaled sharply. His fingers tightened on the edge of the table, his knuckles going white.

"That's an incredible honor," Alden said slowly when Erik didn't speak.

Erik held her gaze, a thousand emotions flying through his blue eyes. Narra reached across the table and took his hand. He squeezed her fingers so tight she thought they might break.

"I-I can't," Erik stuttered. "Not without you."

Narra smiled sadly. "Yes, you can. I need you to do this for me."

"But—"

"This isn't forever," Narra reminded him. "I'll be back as soon as I can."

Erik's gaze welled with unshed tears. "How can you ask me to do this?"

Narra squeezed his hand. "Because you're the only one who can. You're strong and kind and fair. You'll do a far better job at being Guild Master than I ever could. You're the only one I can trust with our family."

Erik yanked her forward suddenly, pulling her into a fierce hug in his lap. He stayed like that, dampening her hair with his tears, his entire body stiff and his grip tight. Alden stood, the legs of his chair screeching across the floor. He folded his arms around both of them. Their warm bodies pressed against hers and she squeezed her eyes shut to hold back the tears burning her eyes.

"This is only goodbye for now," she whispered.

Erik nodded weakly against her and clutched her harder. "You better damn well come back."

Narra chuckled softly. "Not even sea monsters could keep me away."

Erik choked on a laugh, and both Alden and he rumbled against her. She'd never thought the day would come when she'd say goodbye to her best friend, but she had to remind herself it was only goodbye for a while. She *would* see them again, no matter what happened when she found the Sun Goddess.

Narra called her last meeting as Guild Master the next day. It wasn't lost on her that she had been the Guild Master for only a couple short weeks. After everything that had transpired, it seemed silly to say goodbye so soon, but fate had other plans in mind for her.

She stood at the head of the meeting table, the commanders surrounding her, and Erik positioned to her left side like a bodyguard. He'd refused to leave her side for long since last night. After they got the crying out of their systems, they stayed up long into the night despite her growing exhaustion. She told Erik everything he needed to do, the plans she'd begun to make, and how he needed to handle contracts from now on.

Once they were finished, they'd gone to bed. On their way to the Guild, they'd stopped by to inform Jin of the plan. He'd agreed to keep everything a secret. So now, she had to tell the commanders, and she knew they weren't going to be happy.

"I'm leaving," Narra announced. "I've already named the next Guild Master. The position will return to being a secret, but I promise you, this person will hold up the standards of every Guild Master before them."

The commanders blinked at her stupidly, like she might be joking. When she didn't erupt into laughter, the twins were surprisingly the first to protest.

"You're *leaving*?" Claudia snapped. "After all you've done to gain this position, you'll leave us with some *unknown*?"

Narra sighed. She'd let them speak—let them tear her to pieces with their anger. It was the one and only chance they would ever get.

"This is just like you," Klaus growled. "Leaving us to fend for ourselves. Now we'll need to fill your position on the council as well!"

"Actually, you won't," Narra said quickly. "I'm giving my seat to Erik. He is the only person I trust to keep you all in line."

August laughed, while Clint snorted derisively. The rest of them glared at her best friend.

"You want us to just accept this without question?" Claudia growled. "You're playing favorites, just like I knew you would. You can't simply hand someone your position on the council. The position must be *earned* by someone in your faction."

Narra levelled Claudia a *look*. "What faction? I am the only one, so I will do with my position as I see fit. Erik has earned it in my eyes. He shares my love of the Guild and will be a far better mediator than you deserve."

Claudia narrowed her eyes. "What is that supposed to mean?"

Narra ignored her question and looked at the other side of the table. "You all know Erik. You know what he's capable of. He's nearly as strong as I am, and he's well respected by the Guild. No one will question his right to my position as commander."

"She's right," August said. "No one will argue it."

"That's because they've been bed buddies since—"

Narra silenced Klaus with a glare. The commander's eyes widened and then he squinted at her like he was trying to figure something out. He must have noticed her change in eye color. She hadn't thought of a way to explain that, so she quickly looked away from the man.

"I'm leaving tomorrow," Narra said. "There is no stopping it or arguing with my decision."

"Will you return?" Clint asked. He raised an eyebrow, a knowing look in his eyes.

"Someday," she said vaguely.

"I'll be sad to see you go," August said. He stood and reached out to shake her arm. Narra took it before pulling him against her and squeezing him firmly.

"I'll be sad to leave you behind," Narra said.

August cleared his throat as she released him. "We'll all miss you, Rheka."

"Good luck," Narra said. "Don't burn this Guild to the ground without me."

The twins snorted indignantly while the three men on

her right laughed. Even Clint chuckled darkly. Finally she'd gotten a laugh out of that damn man. It had only taken her twenty-five years.

They said their final goodbyes, and then Narra slipped out with Erik on her heels. They met Mika in the sewer and returned to Rova City within the hour. She was determined to keep it a secret from the assassin, though he had to realize something was up by now, especially with the looks everyone was giving her.

By the time they returned to the city, it was nearly dinnertime. She had one last person she had to say goodbye to before she returned home.

It took her several minutes to convince Mika to stay outside, but Erik agreed to stay with the assassin on a rooftop outside the Imperial Palace. That fact seemed to sway him since it was obvious Narra wasn't going anywhere without her best friend.

While they waited outside, Narra flew over the palace's outer wall, right to Asher's window. The latch was still undone, and she slid inside with ease. The room was quiet, but her newfound senses told her that Asher was nearby.

She slipped into the council chamber to find him seated in his usual armchair, a distant look in his eyes as he stared into the fireplace.

The last time she'd been alone with him in his room, he'd tried to convince her to be his secret consort for the rest of their lives. Though her body had recoiled at the idea before, it warmed now at the sentiment behind those words. He cared for her enough that he'd sentence himself to a life with no public wife and no children he could claim as his own.

Narra smiled at the memory. Though she didn't feel the same for him as she had once, part of her would always care for General Asher Grayson.

Asher finally looked up, surprise flashing across his face. "Narra." He stood, his eyes wide. "What are you doing here?" There was hope in his eyes. It killed her that she was about to stomp it out.

"I'm leaving Rova," she said.

Asher's hope died, the spark in his eyes smothered into nothing. He stepped forward and took her hands. "Where are you going?"

"To find out what I am now," she said. She didn't want to be too specific. If anything happened, he could get a hold of Erik. Her best friend would find her.

Asher nodded numbly. "Will I ever see you again?"

Narra smiled ruefully. "Maybe." She didn't want to promise anything. She might return a totally different person, or she might only stop by Rova City every now and then to visit Erik, her uncle, and the Thieves. She had no idea what the future would hold, but she wouldn't lie to him.

Asher nodded, casting his gaze downward. "I love you, Narra."

Her chest squeezed at the broken sound of his voice. He pulled her closer, and wrapped his arms tightly around her. Narra sighed and closed her eyes. She leaned her head against his warm chest and breathed in his sandalwood scent. "I love you too."

His body stiffened against hers. She did love him, or she

had once. He pulled back gently, his eyes filled with unshed tears.

Narra tried to smile, but her lips wouldn't obey.

Asher bent his head and placed a gentle, chaste kiss on her lips. Then he leaned back and released her. "Have a happy life, Asher."

Asher's jaw worked back and forth. Whatever he wanted to say, he held himself back, and she appreciated that. She didn't want to have to deny him again. She wanted to leave like this—like friends.

"Goodbye," she said softly.

Asher nodded, his fists clenching at his sides. He forced his gaze back up to hers. "Goodbye, Narra."

"Ria." Narra's eyes widened in surprise when she returned to her apartment only to find the assassin on the couch. Avalon looked between her and Ria, concern wrinkling her forehead. "Hey, are you all right?"

Ria nodded mutely, her eyes dark and far away. "I'm fine."

Narra glanced over her shoulder at Erik and Mika, who looked like two awkward men about to be faced with feelings. She sighed and took Ria's arm gently, helping her up off the couch. "Let's talk."

She guided Ria to her room, Avalon following close behind. Once they were situated on her bed with the door firmly shut behind them, she took Ria's hand and squeezed.

"Tell me what's wrong," Narra said. She wasn't surprised that she could feel the despair falling off Ria in waves. There was a connection there that she hadn't discovered yet, but the strands of it were tight in her mind, linking her with her new sister.

"I don't know what to do anymore," Ria said. Her voice was flat, conveying no emotion. "Mona's gone. The Ashra I knew is gone. What's left for me?"

Narra exchanged a worried look with Avalon.

"I thought I wanted to live, but maybe it would have been better if I'd died."

Narra squeezed Ria's hand too hard, making the assassin wince. She muttered an apology and loosened her hold. She looked at Avalon, a question in her eyes. Avalon gave her a quick nod, so Narra looked back at the assassin. "We're leaving Rova. Do you want to come with us?"

Ria looked up, a bit of surprise flashing in her dark eyes. "Where are you going?" She paused. "To find Srah?"

Narra smiled and nodded. She couldn't imagine what it was like to lose everyone you knew and loved in one day. She couldn't bear to see Ria like this. "Yes. Come with us if you'd like. We're leaving tomorrow."

Ria stared at her for a few long moments, deliberating. Finally determination set in her gaze, a little bit of the old Ria pushing through. "You're all I have left, Narra." She bit down on her lip. "I'll go with you."

Narra sighed in relief. Every part of her, including all the *others* in her mind, didn't want to leave Ria behind. "We'll figure this out."

Ria nodded.

"Meet us at the City Docks in the morning. Look for the pirate ship," Narra said.

A spark of interest kindled in Ria's eyes, giving Narra hope that Ria would eventually return to old herself. She needed time to grieve, and maybe the best place for her to do that was far away from everything she'd lost.

"A pirate ship?" Ria tilted her head.

"Yes." Narra smiled.

Ria's lips twitched like she might smile. "All right. I'll see you in the morning."

Narra said goodbye for the night and watched the assassin disappear out of her room. Once the door was closed behind her, Avalon turned to her, a curious look in her eyes.

"I'm wondering... what do you plan on doing about your stalker?" Avalon asked.

A laugh burst from Narra's chest. "Mika?"

Avalon shrugged. "Who else?"

Narra leaned against the pirate, and Avalon snaked an arm around her shoulders. "I have a plan to give him the slip. Can you have your ship ready by tomorrow morning?"

Avalon nodded. "What do you need me to do?"

"Be on the ship and have everything ready to go."

Avalon grinned mischievously. "I can do that."

Narra laughed at the glint in Avalon's eye. She was going to enjoy getting rid of Mika *far* too much.

The cold evening air brushed her hair from her shoulders later that night. She sat on the roof, leaning back on her hands with one leg dangling over the edge of the roof. She tilted her face to the sky and inhaled the crisp air.

Her enhanced senses gave her a new appreciation for the world. She could smell the snow in the air and the frost on the breeze. She could feel the cold like tiny pinpricks on her skin and see the millions of stars in the heavens above. She'd never noticed before, but the stars varied in sizes, just like they varied in color. Each one was unique and more mysterious than the one before it.

She had no idea what the stars were, nor did any of the other minds inside of her, which left them a beautiful mystery she wasn't sure she ever wanted to uncover.

"Damn it's getting cold out," Erik hissed out a breath as he stepped off the escape ladder onto the roof. His breath huffed in puffy clouds around his face. His nose was pink and he rubbed his hands together hard. "Aren't you cold?"

Narra smiled and shook her head. She could *feel* the cold, but it didn't bother her. If it could, she wouldn't be sitting outside without a cloak or gloves on. She only wore a blouse, her leather pants, and her usual knee-high boots. Her fingers were bare, and the wind ruffled her clothes, slithering up underneath to tickle her skin, but none of it made her shiver for warmth.

Erik snorted. "I guess godhood has its perks."

He sat down beside her, dangling both of his legs over the edge of the roof. Narra stared at the side of his face as he inspected the sky. Though clouds were forming to block out the stars, he kept looking, a slow smile pulling at the edge of his lips. He knew she was staring, but he let her.

"Do you remember the last time we sat on a roof together?" she asked.

Erik's smile grew. "I don't know, Narra. This is kind of a habit for us."

She chuckled. "Good point."

"The last time we *stood* on a roof side by side might have been during Initiation Day when the Boomers blew up that warehouse in Old Town," Erik guessed.

Narra flashed her teeth in a grin. "That's the time. Back then, did you ever think so much could change so quickly?"

Erik sighed loudly. "Never. I still can't believe that was only a couple of months ago."

Narra hummed her agreement and returned her gaze to the sky. The stars were completely hidden now. She inhaled the cold air. It was going to snow. "We've met so many people and had so many things try to tear us apart, yet we always come back to the rooftops."

Erik finally looked at her, his forehead creased. "It's our safe place."

Narra smiled. "It was always my safe place until you decided you wanted to join too."

Erik tilted his head back and laughed. "You're right. I saw you up here all the time when we were little, and I wanted nothing more than to join you in the clouds."

Her heart clenched. "I'm glad you did."

Tears burned the back of her eyes. She wanted to say she couldn't imagine what her life would have been like without him, but she could. She would have drowned in her loneliness, been eaten alive by her fury, or torn to pieces by her abusive father. Any one of those things could have killed her if she was alone. But with Erik, they were bearable.

"Thank you for following me into the clouds," she said. Tears burned tracks down her face. She swiped at her cheeks until Erik took her hand. She met his eyes, which brimmed with tears of his own.

"You know I'd do it again in a heartbeat," he said. "If you asked me to leave this empire tomorrow, I would. All you have to do is say the word."

Narra smiled sadly and shook her head. Disappointment flashed in his eyes, just as she knew it would. "I won't ask you to do that. Someone needs to hold this country together while I'm gone."

He snorted at her small joke. "Yeah, and we both know your general can't do it."

She winced. Asher wasn't hers—not anymore. "Keep an eye on him, would you?"

Erik nodded quickly, a determined look in his eyes. "I'll miss you, you know."

Narra met his teary gaze. "I'll miss you more."

He barked a teary laugh and wiped his cheeks with the back of his hand. "Impossible."

Narra squeezed his hand. They settled into the comfortable silence she'd always appreciated about her best friend. And as she looked to the sky, snow fell for the first time that year.

She smiled despite the sadness swallowing her. She tilted her head to the sky and let the snowflakes fall onto her cheeks, tiny cold burns slowly peppering her skin. When this all started, winter was just beginning to chill the air, and now it was here. It seemed fitting that she'd be leaving the second it started.

While winter caged the city in snow and ice, she would sail to warmer tides and perhaps finally figure out exactly who she was now that she didn't have the weight of the empire or the Guild on her shoulders.

THE NEXT MORNING, Avalon slipped off early to prepare her crew. Once the pirate had disappeared, Narra ate breakfast casually with her best friend and Mika. He didn't seem any more suspicious than he had yesterday, especially as she meandered around slowly that morning.

She claimed they all needed a few days break—that it

was time to rest up and relax with the worst of things behind them. Mika barely grunted an agreement before shoveling eggs into his mouth.

Narra hid her sly smile with her hand and quietly ate breakfast, all while trying to ignore Erik and Alden's devastated looks. She'd said her goodbyes to her uncle in the dead of night once she'd had her fill of snow and Erik was too freezing to stay outside any longer.

It was hard saying goodbye to the only family she'd ever truly cared for, but she knew that they understood better than anyone why she needed to leave—not only to find out what would happen to her, but where her place in life was now that her job was done.

"It's too bad Avalon couldn't stay," Erik said through a yawn. "She's missing out on a killer breakfast, if I do say so myself."

Mika chuckled, nearly choking on his eggs. Narra smiled. Erik was trying to act normal and make light of things, no matter how much sadness welled in his eyes.

"So humble." Narra flashed a grin.

"Always." Erik winked.

Narra finished the last few scoops of her eggs. The second her plate was clean, Erik's smile fell and his fists shook on the table. They'd already said their goodbyes, and he knew he couldn't say anything if she was going to escape Mika.

No matter how much he wanted to hug her one last time, he couldn't. It broke her heart too.

She cleared her throat and stood. "I guess I'll get ready for the day," she said. Narra received only a few grunts in response as she slipped by them. She gave Erik a quick squeeze on the shoulder before slipping down the hall into her room.

The second the door was closed behind her, her heartbeat sped up. She raced around the room, throwing on her clothes and weapons before yanking her rucksack out from beneath her bed. She'd prepared it last night with Avalon's help and had stowed it away for morning. She couldn't waste any time. Mika was bound to figure out what was going on soon.

Narra tightened the straps of her rucksack on her shoulders before opening her window. Cold air assaulted her face, pushing adrenaline through her veins. She crouched on the windowsill and brandished her grappling hook. She'd miss being able to fly over the city every day, but she had to remind herself this wasn't goodbye forever. She'd return one day.

Steeling her resolve, she aimed at the neighboring building before pressing down hard on the release. Her grappling hook shot forward with a burst of compressed air, flying across the empty street before *thudding* against the chimney. She pulled on the cord to make sure it stuck before she leapt from her windowsill. She freefell for half a second before slamming her thumb down on the retract button.

Her breath was yanked from her lungs as the upward current tore her from her fall and up onto the neighboring building. She released the button and caught her breath on the steeple of the roof. While her cord returned to her fist, she looked over her shoulder at her open window.

When would she see her apartment again? Would it even

be hers? She'd left the deed to the building with Erik, and she'd given him access to every document she owned or had been hidden in her father's mysterious secret room.

A flash of blond hair and blue eyes appeared in the window. Mika's face filled with rage and surprise as he met her gaze. "Death bringer!" he yelled. His fingers shook on the window ledge.

She grinned and shot off her grappling hook again. It didn't matter that he caught on so quickly. There was no beating her pace when it came to flying.

The cord yanked her from the rooftop and again she went sailing through the air. Her heartbeat pounded hard and adrenaline pumped in her veins as she flew over building after building, landing and leaping quicker than she ever had before. She was one with the wind, a bird in the current. She breathed in the cold air until it seared her lungs.

All too soon, she landed on the warehouse across from the City Docks. Her heartbeat slowed as she caught her breath. She slipped down to the alley floor and circled the building until cobblestone gave way to wooden planks. She walked across the docks to Avalon's familiar pirate ship.

Shouts rang through the air, and pirates raced across the deck. A grin pulled at her lips as she walked up the plank to observe the chaos.

It was beautiful in a way—the easy way the crew moved together, slipping and twirling around anyone who ran into their path. They moved almost like dancers—dancers that growled and hissed and spit at each other.

"Narra!" Avalon called from behind the wheel. She had her captain's hat on, but her black curls still billowed in the wind all the same. Excitement filled her eyes, and her chest rose and fell quicker than usual.

Narra climbed over the railing and walked up the steps to join Avalon behind the wheel. She gave Avalon a quick kiss before she saw a shadow move at the edge of her vision. She pulled back to find Ria leaning against the railing, a bag at her feet and pain swirling in her eyes.

"I'm glad you came," Narra said.

Ria only nodded and looked away, staring back at the city.

"We're ready to go," Avalon said. "Are you?"

Narra looked back at the City Docks. No matter how sad she was to say goodbye to the only home she'd ever known, she was also excited about this new adventure with the woman she loved. "I'm ready."

Avalon grinned. She squeezed Narra's hand before turning back to her captain's wheel. "It's time to head back to the sea, gentlemen!" she called to the pirates flying by on the deck below.

Cheers rang from the crew, but they didn't pause. The sails were hoisted and snapped against the wind. The ropes holding them to the dock were pulled back up on deck, and then the wind was tearing them away from Rova City.

Narra's heart leapt as the ship sailed away from the dock. It was slow at first, but then it was as if the wind felt Avalon's excitement because the breeze turned into a great gust of air, sweeping them out into the bay towards the rising sun.

Gold blazed on the surface of the water, setting the sea on fire with its intense rays.

"I think your shadow found you," Ria said.

Narra jumped in surprise and turned back to look at the dock. Mika stood at the edge with his hands on his hips. A laugh bubbled from her throat. He'd almost caught up after all.

Mika shook his head and raised two fingers to his forehead in a salute, and then he turned on his heel and walked back the way he'd come, up the main street into Rova City.

Once the assassin disappeared from sight, her elation slowly faded and nerves rolled in her belly. She turned back around and leaned against the railing to face the sun.

Derrick climbed the steps and nodded at Narra. There was something like respect in his eyes. Maybe he was finally coming around.

Avalon handed off control of her ship to her second-in-command and returned to the railing to lean alongside Narra. She entwined her fingers with Narra's, her thumb rubbing the back of her hand gently. She could feel the jittery excitement of the pirate. It competed with her warring nerves.

There were so many unknowns ahead. So many things she needed to figure out. She was leaving everyone she'd grown up with behind—her family, her Guild, and her best friend.

She'd never imagined a life without them, but she'd never imagined the last few months could have ever happened either.

Avalon squeezed her hand, pulling her attention back to the present. The pirate wrapped a hand in Narra's hair and pulled her forehead against hers. Her smile was sweet and sly all at once. "Are you ready for our journey?"

Narra's heart pounded hard. She heard the double meaning behind her words. This wasn't only a new adventure to places Narra had never been before, she was also in all new territory when it came to Avalon.

She took a deep breath and nodded. Warmth blossomed through her at the happy look dancing in Avalon's eyes. The pirate's smile was infectious.

"More than ready," Narra said confidently.

Avalon grinned like a madwoman and pressed her lips against Narra's, sealing their silent promise to each other with a kiss.

The End

Narra's journey might be over for now, but more stories are coming in the Known World! This Spring, join Avalon's mother, Jacqueline Killian, as she adventures on the high seas of Rupa during a time when bloodsucking creatures ruled the seas.

Join my newsletter to be notified:
http://www.subscribepage.com/p200e3

Thank you so much for joining me on this journey with Narra! This series means so much to me, as does your interest in it! I hope you enjoyed the Clockwork Thief series even half as much as I enjoyed writing it! <3

Whether you enjoyed *Goddess of Death* or not, please consider leaving a review on Amazon, and/or Goodreads! Every review helps get the book in the hands of new readers, and is extremely helpful!

ACKNOWLEDGEMENTS

I can't believe this series has come to an end. I've loved every second of it, especially hearing comments from readers about how much they love Narra, Erik, and the rest of the cast of Clockwork Thief. I appreciate every message from you guys so much. Thank you for coming on this journey with me, and I do hope you'll stick around for my coming series - especially those set in the same world. You never know, Narra and friends might pop up again. ;)

Since this is the last round of acknowledgements I'll ever give for Clockwork Thief, I have a few more people than usual to thank.

First, I'd like to thank Rachel of the Patchwork Press interns for sticking with me for all six of these books. You do incredible work and my books would NOT be the same without you! Then, there is my cover designer on this project, Ravenborn/Anika. She is a designer badass, and I love your work so much, girl!

I'd also like to thank all of the ARC readers who have stuck with me throughout this series. I know we've had some ups and downs, but I am so grateful for every single one of you!

As always, I'd also like to thank the best writing buddies in the entire world, Kellie and Mickey. You ladies inspire me every day, and I couldn't do this without you.

Last, but certainly not least, I'd like to thank my wonderful parents, Bill and Peggy, for supporting me, and proofreading at a moments notice. Thank you guys so much!

Katherine Bogle is the bestselling author of the steampunk phenomenon, QUEEN OF THIEVES, as well as the international bestselling DOMINION RISING series.

She first found success with her debut novel, Haven, which came second in the World's Best Story contest 2015. Since then, she has gone on to release 11 books with one core theme: kick-butt heroines. Though her series may span genres—from fantasy, to steampunk to science fiction—she will always write about strong women overcoming the odds.

Katherine is a lover of all things artistic, including photography, digital painting, and of course, writing. When she isn't working on her next book, she can be found playing video games, binge watching Netflix, or designing book covers.

Join her newsletter for info on upcoming releases, free stuff and more:

https://www.subscribepage.com/p200e3

Follow Katherine for all the latest updates:

katherinebogle.com

AuthorKatherineBogle@outlook.com

facebook.com/AuthorKatherineBogle

twitter.com/KattyB3

instagram.com/katherinebogle

goodreads.com/katherinebogle

bookbub.com/profile/katherine-bogle

CLOCKWORK THIEF

Queen of Thieves

Daughter of Chaos

King of Empires

Empress of Annihilation

Harbinger of War

Goddess of Death

CHRONICLES OF WARSHARD

Haven

Savages

Ashen

Fyre: *A Short Story Collection*

The Blood Amulet: *A Short Story*

DOMINION RISING

The Aldar Dominion

The Zahkx Alliance

The Darri Commission

Epilogue: *A Novelette*

The Stowaway Experiment: *A FREE Short Story*

The Smugglers Legion: *A Short Story*

FIND OUT MORE ON

KATHERINEBOGLE.COM

Made in the USA
Middletown, DE
22 June 2019